BACKSTORY

Journalists Off the Record

WILLIAM SARGENT

PRAISE FOR WILLIAM SARGENT'S BOOKS

Shallow Waters; A Year on Cape Cod's Pleasant Bay (Houghton Mifflin)

"With his fine descriptions and lucid explanations, Sargent joins the company of Lewis Thomas and Stephen Jay Gould as a first-rate interpreter of modern science."
—Publisher's Weekly

"It is a gem of Natural History… the best introduction to the original environment of the New England coast."
—Dr. E. O. Wilson, Harvard University

A joy to read."
—The Washington Post

A Year in the Notch; Exploring the White Mountains

"A Great Read! Sargent takes us on a raucous jaunt through the New England forest, to see the big picture with unclouded eyes. A true biologist he examines everything in sight and counts it relevant, connecting it with seamless prose into the rational new picture. It's a powerful boost to the new Nature religion that references us to Life on Earth."
—Dr. Bernd Heinrich

Storm Surge; A Cape Cod Village Battles the Rising Atlantic

It's science writing that reads like a novel, with all the page-turning excitement of a thriller." — William Martin

"Sargent can turn an event as mundane as a rising tide into poetry. This is a book for everyone who loves the shore, especially Cape Cod." —The Boston Globe

The Year of the Crab; — Marine Animals in Modern Medicine

"If you only have time for one book about life-death dramas played to the sound of crashing waves, about new science and the old sea, about Nobel prizes, squid brains and sex orgies on Cape Cod
· beaches, then this book is for you."
—Dr. A.A. Moscona, Journal of the American Medical Association

Terror by Error? The Covid Chronicles

"An intriguing assemblage of scientific stories, a delightfully captivating read."
—Kirkus Reviews

Backstory
Journalists Off the Record

First Edition
Copyright © 2023 by William Sargent

Published by
Singer Sargent Productions

Print ISBN: 978-1-960299-00-0

Printed in the United States of America

OTHER TITLES BY WILLIAM SARGENT

"Shallow Waters; A Year on Cape Cod's Pleasant Bay"
— Winner of the Pen and Boston Globe's Winship Award.

"Storm Surge; A Coastal Village Battles Sea Level Rise."

"World on Edge"

"Plum Island, 4,000 Years on a Barrier Beach"

"20,000 Years on the Merrimack River"

"Crab Wars, A Tale of Horseshoe Crabs, Ecology and Human Health"

"The House on Ipswich Marsh"

"A Year in the Notch; Exploring New England's White Mountains"

"North of Boston, The Edge of a Warming World"

"Terror by Error?"

TABLE OF CONTENTS

ACKNOWLEDGMENTS

I have been extremely fortunate to have spent most of my career surrounded by researchers, scientists, and medical doctors. At the same time, my writing habit has allowed me to meet other science writers in the field, in labs, in editorial meetings, and over late-night beers and cocktails.

The more I talked to my colleagues the more I realized that no one particular path led them to science writing. Some came from academic research, others from medicine, some started as cub reporters, and a few even came from schools of journalism.

As science writers, they were people fascinated with the miracles of life, existence, and our universe. They had traveled the world and met scientists immersed in research with the God-like potential to reshape the world. They had written about issues that will determine whether our species, even our planet, will survive.

It is to honor this field and these writers that I have written this book. Dozens of them have told me their stories and helped me write this novel. I am particularly grateful to Dr. Brown for her help and inspiration and to all the good people at Munn Avenue Press for reading and rereading the manuscript in its many iterations.

Finally, I would like to caution the reader that you may think you recognize ghostly apparitions of some of these writers in these pages but that would just be a happy illusion because the characters in this book are fictitious and any resemblance to persons living or dead is purely coincidental.

CHAPTER 1

The Editorial Meeting

Boston, Massachusetts

11 AM: Finbar Muldoon switched on the Zoom meeting. The first person to sign on was Gregor McFadden. Finbar liked McFadden. He had signed up for covering the war in Ukraine after breaking up with his girlfriend.

"Got your running shoes, Greg?"

"Sure do!"

"Where are you?"

"Can't tell you. I'm huddled underground in an undisclosed location in Kyiv. My biggest problem is keeping all my batteries charged. If the power goes out I'm screwed."

"What do you have for us?"

"I had been planning to make my way into Belarus to see if I can find out what happened to those soldiers who had collected radioactive souvenirs from their stay in Chernobyl. But now it sounds like the Russians have upped their bombing in anticipation of their push into the Donbas. I can hear the sirens and feel the detonations even down here."

"Be careful."

"Don't worry. I will."

"Do you think the video of the sinking of the *Moskva* taken from the Russian tugboat is real?"

"Absolutely, you can even hear someone saying 'what the fuck do you think you're doing?'"

"Yes, they seem to drop as many f-bombs as we do on Morrissey Boulevard."

"You can see the *Moskva* davits hanging empty. So they must have abandoned ship before it sank. But the word here is that several hundred sailors were wounded."

"See if you can confirm that. In the meantime do you think you can get closer to the Donbas?"

"Petra seems to think so."

"So who's Petra?"

"She is an ambulance driver who has been helping me get around Kyiv."

"Oh. Okay, I'll see if I can't get you on the front page and hold open a window for any photographs. Your colleagues are jealous you're getting so many stories above the fold."

"They are welcome to come if you can pry 'em out of Donovan's bar."

"Ok, see what you can get and whatever you do stay safe."

11:05 AM: "Glad the rest of you could join us.

We have the two biggest stories of our lives just outside these bullet-proof windows. Covid is killing off humanity almost as fast as Russia is killing off the Ukrainians.

Sylvia, do you have anything for us over there in STAT?"

Sylvia was a graduate of Harvard Medical School but after her residency, she had decided that she could do more for medicine by writing about it for the Boston Globe's sister organization STAT, established to cover New England's burgeoning health and biotech industries.

"I do. I want to dig into the Omicron story. Talk to Dr. Lessells in South Africa. He's the guy who thinks the Omicron variant came from a single immunocompromised HIV patient."

"See if you can get the next flight out. I'm afraid it might be close to Christmas."

"That's alright. Remember I'm Jewish. A Jewish Christmas is ordering take-out Chinese and watching a good movie. I'll be fine."

"OK, we also have this billion-dollar blizzard and freeze in California. Thousands of people are trapped in their cars and could die from carbon monoxide poisoning. The storm may even rebuild their snowpack. Ericka, you're our doom and gloom gal. Can you unpack all that?"

"Doom and gloom person Finbar, doom and gloom person!

And no, I'm sick and tired of covering these damn disaster du jour stories. I want to fly to the Arctic to see the temperature changes firsthand."

"Whereabouts exactly?"

"Place called Verkhoyansk, Siberia."

"Siberia! You want me to pay you to fly to Siberia?"

"Just get me to Moscow. The Russian Academy of Sciences will take over from there."

"This better be good."

"Oh it will, it will."

CHAPTER 2

Verkhoyansk, Siberia
April 23, 2022

Ericka was glad to be back on solid ground even if it was just melting permafrost. How was she going to get along with this group of vodka-swilling scientists?

Things had not gone well from the start. The windshield of the bus the Russian Academy of Sciences had chartered to show the American scientists around Moscow had exploded in the frigid air, and the scientists, the handlers, and their embedded journalist ended up huddled for warmth in a massive group hug in the back of the bus. It was the first time Ericka had ever seen a Russian, let alone been hugged by one.

Their driver met them at the Verhoyansk airport and they piled into his government issue Volga. As they approached the ancient Cossack fort, a statue with two fifteen-foot-high mammoth tusks loomed into their headlights.

"That is to commemorate that Verkhoyansk once held the all-time record for the coldest temperature in the Northern Hemisphere. It was minus 38 degrees Centigrade, that is minus 90 degrees in your capitalistic Fahrenheit system," intoned their handler. The head of the American delegation guffawed.

"But it was crazy last year. On June 20, 2021, the temperature rose to 100.4 degrees Fahrenheit, almost a 200-degree temperature range in this single location."

"Where do the tusks come from?"

"Along the banks of the Yana River just outside of town. The climate is now so mild the permafrost has melted so you can find the bodies of mammoths being scoured out of the new bends in the river."

"Haven't you had trouble with illegal tusk hunters?"

"No, no. No trouble at all!"

Dmitri Pitulko whispered into Ericka's ear, "That's pure bullshit. Looters have ruined several mammoth cemeteries. It's as bad as the illegal amber trade in Kaliningrad. They use pumps to melt the permafrost with bursts of hot water. Last October six starving looters had to be airlifted out of Bolyshoy Lyakhovsky Island in the Siberian chain. Serves them right!

By the way, we have already changed our nickname for you," Dmitri continued. "We used to call you 'period' for your short size. Now we call you 'exclamation point' for your sharp questions!"

"Does Academik Pitulko wish to share something with the rest of us?" glowered the handler.

Ericka continued, "Aren't you concerned about what climate change will do to your agriculture?"

"Far from it. We look forward to growing wheat in Siberia and shipping it out of our Arctic ports to Asia."

"Sounds like Lysenkoism all over again," retorted Ericka.

The Russian scientists enjoyed seeing their handler squirm. Lysenko had set back Soviet science and agriculture several decades.

The handler pushed on. Ericka had started to call him Vlad in her notes.

"Our icebreakers can already break through the thin summer ice. It used to be 10 meters tall, but now it is full of polynya."

"What's the English word for polynya?"

"Holes, holes! You don't have an English word or polynya in your limited colonial language!"

"Oh God, this is going to be a long trip," Ericka muttered into her recorder. Dmitri smiled into his beard.

CHAPTER 3

Shanghaied

Hong Kong, PRC
April 27, 2022

"Control your soul's desire for freedom. Do not open the window or sing."

Message broadcast from surveillance
drone over Shanghai, China.
April 25, 2022

Hong Kong was the closest Sylvia could get to Shanghai, but she had been able to make phone contact with Dr. John Chang, an American lecturer at the Shanghai Medical College of Fudan University.

"Dr. Chang, first of all, can you tell me what the last month has been like in Shanghai?"

"Horrible. Absolutely horrible. If you test positive for Covid you are forced to stay in huge quarantine facilities with no hot water, little food, and the lights are on 24 hours a day.

And it's not much better if you are in your own apartment. You can't get out to buy your own food and there is nobody to deliver other food because they are also in lockdown. It is like one big prison, and now it might spread to Beijing. I'm sure you have seen the videos of people attacking the police and shouting out their windows."

"Only for as long as they are up on Weibo."

"Yes, the government has been diligent about taking them down. But the most shocking thing to me is that here we have the largest city in China that was running like clockwork a month ago. Now we have 25 million people scrounging for food."

"But I understand that you were initially in favor of the zero-Covid policy, and now you are against it. Can you explain that?"

"Well, when Covid first broke out, the Chinese government was able to step in and largely contain it. But in America, we were floundering around sending mixed messages and our cases soared."

"I remember."

"Yes, it looked like China's zero-Covid policy was much more successful than anything the West could do, and

it became the Party's shining example of how much better their system was than ours. They believed in their ideology so much they decided to continue to rely on their short-term zero-Covid policy as well as on their own homegrown vaccines even though they knew their vaccines were less effective than America's vaccines. Meanwhile, we were preparing for the long haul with our own messenger RNA vaccines."

"Yes, my editor wrote that it was 'freaking awesome we developed our vaccines in less than a year.'"

"I read that, even over here!"

"Yes, it got much more attention than anything else STAT has written."

"Isn't that always the way?"

"If I mentioned the 1958 Waste Sparrow Campaign, would you know what I am referring to?"

"Of course. That was Mao's plan to rid China of sparrows because each sparrow eats the equivalent of 4 pounds of rice a year. Cadres of people ran through the cities and towns beating drums and lighting fireworks so the sparrows couldn't land in their nests. Eventually, the birds would fall out of the air, exhausted, and their bodies would be carted away. The Polish embassy refused to let anyone in their embassy compound, but their sparrows also died because people surrounded the embassy banging pots and drums."

"And eventually all the sparrows died?"

"Yes, all the sparrows died, but what Mao failed to realize was that sparrows also ate insects, and without predators, China soon had a plague of locusts that led to the Great Famine in which 45 million people died."

"Horrible!"

"Yes, horrible and most of them had terrible deaths. People would dig into mud mines to eat the clay. As soon as their stomachs absorbed water, the clay would congeal as hard as cement and they would die an excruciatingly painful death."

"And the party couldn't reverse the policy because they would have to admit they were wrong."

"Indeed, the perfect case of ideology trumping pragmatism, and we are seeing it again with their zero-Covid policy."

"But let's open this up a bit. China has been busily cozying up to Russia after its invasion of Ukraine. Why would Xi Jinping want to jeopardize China's trade with the West and tether himself to an international pariah like Putin? I always think of China as being more pragmatic and less ideological than that."

"That's because you don't understand the Chinese system. The People's Party takes its ideology very seriously."

Sylvia smiled. Her interviewees seldom disagreed with her.

"You have to understand that China is not a one man one rule country like Putin's Russia. Xi Jinping could never declare war by himself. The Communist party simply wouldn't allow it."

"I see. Really, really, interesting John. Thank you so much. I look forward to getting back to you about future stories."

"Yeah if I still have a job!"

CHAPTER 4

The Donbas, Ukraine
April 28, 2022

The time of crocuses had come and gone, and the fields and hedgerows of the Donbas were turning green.

Gregor was enjoying no longer seeing the charred tanks and bombed out buildings of Kyiv. He liked the view from Petra's ambulance on its way to pick up the victim of a bombing attack.

Petra gripped the wheel and stared intently ahead. She was sticking to the country back roads to avoid any Russian checkpoints. Gregor marveled at her quiet resolve as an EMT.

"Your mother gave you sandwiches and kissed you goodbye as if she were seeing you off to college instead of driving into a war zone."

"Yes, I'm her only daughter. She is quite hysterical that I'm doing this."

"I can imagine. But what are those trees blooming up there?"

"We call them burying trees. In the old days, it was too cold to dig graves in the winter, so our ancestors would save all the dead bodies until spring when the trees bloomed. That signaled that the ground had melted enough so you could bury the dead."

"Bittersweet to name something so beautiful after something so sad."

"Everything is bittersweet in Ukraine, even our trees."

"We have similar trees at home, but we call them shadbush because they bloom when fish called shad start to swim up our rivers and streams."

"You name your trees after fish, how funny. You know we Ukrainians are famous for our trees. My father used to drive us to the Carpathian Mountains just so we could see the forests. There is a place called the Tunnel of Love that is cut through a tall dense stand of pine trees."

"You know I used to write about nature back at home."

"You did? Why did you ever leave to come here?"

"I was in a kind of pause in my life. I was working on a book about New England wildlife and asked a photographer if she could help me get photographs. We would spend all day exploring the fields and forests and especially the dunes and beaches of an island near home."

"Gradually I realized I was what we call 'head over heels in love'. I couldn't take my eyes off her, even though I was married.

But there was always a problem. Whenever we got close she would back away. She had had a difficult life but I always felt she could learn to love again, but she never did."

"That's so sad."

"And hurtful. On the exact same day my divorce came through, she dumped me and boasted about it online."

"How cruel."

"I was devastated, but finally realized how toxic the relationship had actually been.

I needed a change, so when my former editor asked me if I wanted to cover your war, I agreed. So here I am driving into combat, and you know what? It feels safer than falling in love again."

"Haha! Here's the address where we are supposed to pick up the wounded civilian but I don't see anybody around. We'll have to go in and search the building."

As she spoke a shell slammed into the structure.

"Be careful, the bastards often shell twice. One time to wound any civilians, and a second time to kill any rescuers."

But after searching through the rubble they had still not found the victim. Then Petra's phone rang.

"Where the fucks are you? I called half an hour ago!"

"Where the fuck are you? You said 14 Donbas Road and nobody's here."

"Not 14 Donbas Road, 40 Donbas Road! We are hiding in the vestibule."

"Roger that, we'll be right there."

Once they arrived at the correct address, Gregor watched as Petra and Yuri, the unit's emergency technician, loaded the wounded man into the ambulance and hooked him up to an IV. The medicine had its effect, but Gregor could see it was Petra's warm smile and soothing assurances that really calmed him down.

"Yes, I'm just the technician," said Yuri. "She is the true healer."

CHAPTER 5

Grain War

Punjab, India
May 1, 2022

"This heat wave is testing the limits of human survivability."

Chandri Kumar, India's
Glasgow Conference representative

Ericka figured that she had just visited the coldest place on earth, so she should visit the hottest, and right now the hottest place on earth was Punjab. Northern India had just had its hottest April since records had been started 122 years ago. Temperatures across the border in Pakistan had risen to over 120 degrees Fahrenheit.

The pavement was melting when Dr. Kumar met Ericka at the train station.

"Welcome to what's left of 'The Grain Bowl.' How was your trip?"

"Difficult. I couldn't get a connection from Delhi."

"Yes I understand they have taken over 650 passenger trains offline so they can haul coal to the power stations. We have been having massive blackouts throughout the country. Refrigerators and air conditioning won't work, and hundreds of people have already died from heat exposure, and schools and offices have shut down."

"So that's why you voted to phase down, not end, coal use at the Glasgow Conference."

"Ah, now I recognize you, that American journalist who kept asking such annoying questions. You really have too much freedom of the press in your country!

You see ours is what your engineers would call a wicked hard problem. We know burning coal is the worst thing you can do to heat the planet, but it is all we can afford."

"But global warming is destroying your best cash crop. I saw acre upon acre of wheat shriveling up in the fields."

"And it will only get hotter until the monsoons come in late May. We expect to lose half of our wheat harvest this year."

"I understand this was the year you wanted to expand your sales into places like the Middle East and Africa."

"But now the government will have to buy 25 million tons of wheat just to feed our own people.

So you see, Putin is waging a grain war and we are on the frontlines."

"How so?"

"When Ukraine was still part of the Soviet Union it produced more wheat than any other country. They are only first now because American farmers can make more money planting corn to make ethanol and soybeans to sell to China."

"Yes, unbelievable that we put having cheap gas before producing food."

"So now Ukraine is the fifth largest grower of wheat, and Putin doesn't want the competition. He wants Russia to be the only country able to ship wheat out of the Black Sea cheaply. That is why he is trying to destroy ports like Mariupol and Odessa, to make Ukrainian wheat too expensive to export."

"Diabolical!"

"Indeed, this heat wave is testing the limits of human survivability."

"Nonsense, it is we humans who are testing the limits of our planet."

"Touché, my dear Ericka, touché. We must continue this conversation over dinner tonight."

"Not on your life, Dr. Kumar, not on your life!"

CHAPTER 6

The Iceberg Simulation

Washington, D.C.
May 5, 2022

"Every time we turn it on an angel dies."
Colin Carlson co-designer
of the Iceberg Simulation

Sylvia twisted her long blond hair into a bun. She didn't want any stray nightclub hair to reduce her credibility with the two young researchers who had just released their first scientific paper. She joined Bill and Erick in their cramped home office near George Washington University.

"In my line of work the only dumb question is the one you never asked, so can I ask a dumb question?"

"Like is the earth really the center of the universe or how did the continents drift apart? Some of the greatest discoveries in science came from asking dumb questions … others from making mistakes."

"OK then, why are so many of my friends suddenly coming down with Covid? A year ago, it was always someone you just read about."

"You're right. A year ago the virus was only being spread by a few people at super spreader events. Our new crop of variants are much more contagious."

"So we are all spreaders now."

"Yes we are all spreaders now, so no your question wasn't dumb at all. It was to answer a similar dumb question that we designed the Iceberg Simulation. We wanted to know if climate change had a hand in creating this pandemic and would it lead to more."

"Why did you call it the Iceberg Simulation?"

"Because we soon realized we are only seeing the tip of the iceberg. We see viruses jumping from animals like bats and mice to animals like birds, deer, pigs, monkeys, and on to us humans. But they are only the tip of the iceberg.

There are over 3,000 species of animals harboring over 40,000 species of viruses that are migrating to cooler climates because of climate change. When those animals come together we can expect to see approximately 300,000 interactions that will lead to the possibility of 15,000 spillover events, any one of which can lead to one or more pandemics."

"And you see this each time you run the simulation?"

"Yes, the simulation shows that mammalian viruses have already been reshuffled so much by such interactions that they can't be undone even if we stopped carbon emissions tomorrow.

So this era we call the Anthropocene because of our power over the earth, should really be called the Pendemicene because of viruses' power over us."

"But we have the ability to stop them, right?"

"We're not sure. We just spent billions of dollars vaccinating most of the world's population and still over 16 million people died. What would happen if that started happening every year with multiple viruses?"

"I suppose it could wipe out the human species but then it would wipe out the viruses as well."

"Not necessarily. They could just retreat back into their reservoir species and wait to see if the remnant populations of humans would bounce back to overpopulate the earth again."

"Hmm pretty damn unnerving."

"Yes, this virus has us all scratching our heads."

CHAPTER 7

Editorial Meeting

Boston, Massachusetts
May 9, 2022

Gregor, Finbar, and Sylvia were already online when Ericka activated her video.

Finbar: "Welcome to the Zoom meeting Ericka, so glad you could join us."

Ericka: "You mean where we are all locked in like little prisoners in Plato's Cave where we can only see flickering shadows but not scientific reality?"

Finbar: "A little grumpy this morning, Ericka?"

Ericka: "I had a very late night last night."

Sylvia: "Do tell!"

Ericka: "Not a chance Sylvia, not a chance."

Finbar: "OK, OK. Let's get down to business. Can we do anything on the Supreme Court's recent decisions?"

Ericka: "Nobody can do anything with the Supreme Court."

Sylvia: "Except pack it!"

Finbar: "Well, we can't do that. But we can look at how their decisions are affecting our beats. Sylvia, how about you?"

Sylvia: "Well it's pretty obvious they are making it impossible to protect women's health and the Justice Department's banning the CDC's mask mandate has made it impossible to protect human health."

Finbar: "How about climate, Ericka?"

Ericka: "Their decisions on private property rights have made it impossible for states to protect people from things like coastal erosion and forest fires. If a state writes a law that prohibits a developer from building a house on an eroding beach, the state has to pay for their lost revenue. States don't want to do it because they don't want to go broke.

The problem is that our legal system is set up to protect human beings. The same is true for capitalism and communism and any other "ism" you can think of. They are all set up to benefit humans and right now humans are the problem. There is no system for protecting the planet from ourselves."

Finbar: "What about this press release that the government is going to provide 2.5 billion dollars to suck carbon dioxide out of the air? It sounds like science fiction."

Ericka: "It is. What, just so we can continue to drive, fly, have too many babies, and have all the latest electronic gadgets?

It's all a big show to make people think we can build our way out of this environmental mess, to make them think we can just switch fuels, drive electric cars and everything will be hunky dory."

Gregor: "It's true. Nobody has been willing to make real sacrifices except in Ukraine. They are making real sacrifices so they can continue to live under a system of government they believe in. Perhaps their sacrifices will be an example for the rest of the world."

Ericka: "I plan to drop out and run a conch farm. Using my knowledge and labor to produce food that doesn't require artificial food, energy, or fresh water, just turtle grass, sun, and a nice clean estuary. Spend my days snorkeling through turtle grass, checking on my flocks."

Finbar: "Ok but what are you going to do for next week? Fly off to the Arctic again?"

Ericka: "Nope, I'm gonna think globally but write locally. I plan to take a boat out to Muskegat Island off Nantucket. Researchers have found that seals on the tiny island are safe from Great White Sharks, but they are picking up coronaviruses from birds and they might be able to pass on to humans. It kind of lines up with Sylvia's story about the Iceberg Simulation."

Finbar: "Ok sounds like a good local story, Ericka. Gregor what about you? Has the Ukraine dropped off the front page?"

Gregor: "Ukraine Finbar. Ukraine. Are you some sort of revanchist? Putin's Victory Day Speech was such a nothing burger. Pretty defensive, almost contrite really. Trying to say that the West was preparing to take back Crimea."

Finbar: "Do we have any evidence that that was the case?"

Gregor: "Nothing that I have heard. It can best be termed a rumor that sprang out of Putin's pandemic-enhanced paranoia."

Finbar: "So if there is nothing there, what can you give us?"

Gregor: "I was thinking I might travel with Petra again. She has some friends whose husbands are troops still trapped in the Mariupol steel plant."

Ericka: "Oh going out with Petra again, Greggie? Sounds like things are getting serious."

Gregor: "Give me a break Ericka!"

Finbar: "OK, OK. So Sylvia is going to look into the SCOTUS decisions, and perhaps come up with an editorial. Ericka will report on seals and Gregor will interview the wives of troops trapped in Mariupol. You have your assignments- let's go get 'em!"

CHAPTER 8

Manganese Nodules

The Clarion-Clipperton Fracture Zone
500 Miles South of Hawaii
May 11, 2022

Ericka liked the tall athletic Trinidadian woman who huddled beside her as they peered through the forward porthole of their snub-nosed submersible. Outside, plankton flashed bluish-green orbs of annoyance as the large metallic creature drifted down through their swirling clouds of bioluminescence.

"It feels like we are descending through a blizzard of plankton."

"We are," said Anna Diva as the waters outside slowly shifted from light blue, to aqua, to deep purple and violet.

"Speaking of blizzards, you better wriggle into your long johns and woolen hat. The water temperature will be just above freezing by the time we reach the bottom."

"When will that be?"

"About an hour. We are essentially in free fall."

"So we have plenty of time to get to know each other."

Diva flashed an infectious smile, "First tell me why you decided to write this story. Not too many people know about deep-sea mining."

"Actually I heard about it at my first job. In 1975 I was working for the Sierra Club at the Law of the Sea Conference in Venezuela, but a Quaker group was paying half my salary. The problem was that the Sierra Club wanted to protect the oceans, but the Quaker Group wanted to create something called 'The Enterprise', an international entity established to exploit deep-sea mining 'for the benefit of all mankind.'"

"Don't you mean promote?"

"Nope I mean exploit, that's what they called it as well."

"Telling the truth for a change! "

"Yes and The Enterprise became the International Seabed Authority in Jamaica.

And they still have the same problem. They are set up to both protect the deep sea and to manage the mining.

Classic case of the fox guarding the chicken coop.

It was fine as long as nobody had the money or was interested in mining the ocean. But now international companies think they can make a killing mining cobalt from the seafloor, rather than have kids dig it up by hand in places like Afghanistan and the Congo Republic.

Promoters say that deep-sea mining is the way we are going to manufacture all the cobalt-based electronics, batteries and electric cars that will usher in the new era of sustainable green technology. If not the era of nice green sawbucks!

But here, you can see for yourself. The bottom is just looming into view. There are the manganese nodules."

"Why they look just like Idaho potatoes!"

"But each one is a conglomerate of manganese, iron, nickel and cobalt. And each one is also a million years old."

"So mining them is certainly not sustainable."

"Absolutely not. And look what is between them. Cnidarians, jellyfish-like animals with eight-foot-long tentacles, sea cucumbers that look like cuddly teddy bears, sharks that glow in the dark, and glass sponges that have been around since the Stone Age."

"How many of those species have been identified?" asked Ericka as their submersible started its ascent back to the surface.

"Less than ten percent. That is why scientists like me have been calling for a moratorium on deep-sea mining, so we have time to clarify any potential problems before we charge ahead."

"But the head of the Seabed Authority calls your moratorium 'anti-science, anti-intellectual anti-development and anti-international law.'"

"He would say that he's an international lawyer. The problem is that we don't have enough scientific information to make informed decisions about how to manage this activity.

Scrapping the ocean floor could permanently affect the communities of animals that live on the sea bottom. But the greatest impact could come from the plumes of sediment caused by dumping mining tailings back into the sea. The toxic tailings can kill off zooplankton over large swaths of the Pacific Ocean, which is the biological pump that naturally sequesters millions of tons of carbon every year."

"Are comments like that the reason you are no longer invited to the Seabed's workshops?"

"For sure!"

"So ultimately it comes down to whether you think we should engineer the planet for the benefit of one species, ourselves; or for the benefit of the myriad of interconnected organisms that make up our life-supporting biosphere?"

"It is clear that the biosphere can exist quite happily without our species. The question is, can we exist without the biosphere?"

"I guess the only person who thinks we can is Elon Musk, and that uber-Star Trek fan doesn't care because he thinks he can fly away and screw up another planet."

"This has been fun. But look here we are back in the sun on the surface."

"Time flies when you're having fun."

CHAPTER 9

The Sniper

Kharkiv, Ukraine
May 13, 2022

Petra met Gregor outside his underground apartment in Kyiv.

"Well good morning! Where did you get this car? "

"It's my mother's Skoda, a hybrid. We bought it before the war. Now it is useful when both gas and electricity can disappear at any moment."

"She lent it to you to take to the front?"

"I told her we were going for a picnic outside Kyiv."

"You devil! Where are we going?"

"Kharkiv. I want you to meet one of my old school friends. We used to go clubbing together. She is very beautiful, always flirting with the boys."

"What does she do now?"

"I'll let her tell you when we meet her. What did you think of Putin's speech?"

"Not much. I had expected him to declare war so he could draft more conscripts."

"Yes, we rained on his parade. Is that how you say it?"

"Ha. Quite literally in this case."

"It is the third time we rained on his parade. First we stopped him from taking Kyiv. Our soldiers even found formal parade clothes in some of the Russian's tanks. They had planned to wear them in their victory parade."

"Then you destroyed the *Moskva*."

"Yes, our guys harassed their gunners with Bayraktar drones until they finally took the bait and tried to shoot them down. As soon as their gunners locked onto the drones, our Neptune missiles hit them from the other side of the ship. The Russian sailors never even saw the missiles that sank them."

"What was the third time?"

"Just yesterday. Our reconnaissance drones captured several tanks and supply trucks creeping across a pontoon bridge over the Siverskyi Donets River. We blew up the bridge and dozens of their tanks and trucks. Now they have retreated behind the river, so our artillery can freely bomb their supply lines."

"Why do you think the Russians keep sacrificing so many soldiers?"

"Our intelligence guys think the orders are coming right from the top."

"Putin?"

"Yes he is desperate for some kind of victory."

"How did you think he looked during the parade?"

"In my professional opinion, quite awful. I've seen a lot of sick people and he is one sick puppy!"

"Where do you learn such expressions?"

"One of our medical teachers came from the Chan School of Public Health at Harvard. He was from the south. He called it your Duke of the North."

"Ha! Yes, Putin looked very cold during the parade, he even had a blanket draped over his legs."

"That was to hide his tremors. He has them in both his hands and legs. Often you can see him clasping his hands and tapping his feet."

"Do you think he has Parkinsons?"

"I've heard he has blood cancer and was scheduled to have stomach surgery after Victory Day."

"So he might be unconscious right now. If so they would make sure we would never hear about it until well after the fact."

Petra turned down an abandoned road. They were close enough to the front to hear the artillery lobbing shells at supply lines inside Russia.

"Well, here we are. This is Alexandra's unit. They are

bivouacked over there under the trees. But only walk down this path. There may still be landmines."

Alexandra came out to meet them. She had long brown hair, deep dimples, and leathery skin from spending so much time in the sun.

"How the hell are you Petra and who is this f-ing American?"

"This is Gregor McFadden, a writer from Boston. He wants to know how your counterattack went."

"It was our fastest most efficient strike yet. The Russians just fell back. They even blew up three bridges while retreating which makes us think they are not planning on coming back."

"What exactly do you do with this unit?"

"Our specialty is killing Russian generals. We're snipers!"

"Whoa, how did you get into the sniper business?"

"During basic training, they took all of us to the firing range and I hit my first three bullseyes: plink, plink, plink!"

They gave me three more rounds and it was the same thing: plink, plink, plink. My commanding officer pulled me aside and told me I should join our Special Forces sniper unit."

"How did they train you to be a sniper?"

"First they taught us all about camouflage."

"You must have loved that. You always loved putting on make-up," said Petra.

"Still do!"

"You always called it your war paint."

"Still is!"

"We also learned how to sleep very still in the forest. Sometimes we sleep only meters from the Russians' trenches. Sometimes we sleep in trees."

"How about your equipment? It must be very heavy."

"It is. Our rifles are very long, heavy, and equipped with high-powered sights. We can pick off a tank commander a mile away.

I always look for gray hair, which means a senior officer has been dumb enough to stand up in his tank. I'm still waiting to bag my first general. The drone guys pick off most of them first."

On the way home Gregor asked, "Is Alexandra single?"

"Very single. If you want to have a lot of sex and no commitment, then she is your girl."

"Sounds like fun."

"Sad really. As soon as you start to get close she backs away."

"Perhaps it makes her a good sniper."

"But a bad lover."

"How do you know?"

"Because I'm a good lover!"

CHAPTER 10

The Yellow Tags

Baltimore, MD
May 15, 2022

Sharks circled around Sam and Sylvia amidst the whooshing sounds of pumps and filters in the dimly lit basement of the Baltimore Aquarium.

"Are you sure we are safe here?" asked Sylvia.

"Yup, a friend of mine is the curator, and he gave me the key."

"So, tell me why you contacted the paper?"

"I used to be head of manufacturing operations at Bio Solutions not far from here."

"Didn't Trump give them the Operation Warp Speed contract to produce the Covid vaccines?"

"Exactly, we were in over our heads from the start. But our executives had 'ins' with the government that went back to 9/11 and the war in Iraq."

"Who were the executives?"

"Well, one of the big ones was a Lebanese businessman whose father had been making an anthrax vaccine for the Saudis. Others were former high level government employees."

"Wait a minute. I did a story about that Lebanese guy. It was after 9/11 and we were preparing to invade Iraq. The CIA was saying that the Iraqis might use anthrax as a biological weapon. At the time the only anthrax vaccine the U.S. had come from a poor little pinpricked horse living in Michigan's public health department lab."

"That's right, Douad Al Hambra was the guy."

"I kept trying to set up interviews with him not far from here, but just before I was about to get on a plane, he would call to tell me he had to fly to London for a business trip or Europe for a wedding."

"That would be him."

"Then a few hours after I hung up the phone there would be a news story about a man and his 16-year-old companion who had just assassinated another victim within blocks of Douad's office near Fort Detrick, Maryland."

"That's where the military was working on biological weapons."

"Yup, the two shooters killed about a dozen people."

"I remember that."

"One of them was an agent investigating the scientist at Fort Detrick who was suspected of sending anthrax through the mail."

"The anthrax mailer!"

"Precisely. I finally got so paranoid I called the FBI to ask if they thought there could be any connection between the anthrax mailings and the assassinations. I figured no one would ever get back to me but the agent in charge of the investigation called back ten minutes later."

"What happened?"

"Well, we walked through the sequence of events, but the times never quite lined up. But I was very impressed they took my call so seriously."

"I understand the FBI gets most of their leads from observant bystanders who see something strange."

"The way we get ours from whistleblowers."

"That would be me I suppose."

"Precisely just what did you see at BioSolutions?"

"I had long standing problems with the company. Back in 2020, I wrote a memo to the senior executives saying they had serious quality control problems.

It only got worse when we were awarded the Warp Speed contract. What really kept me up at night were conditions at the Bayside facility."

"Did they do something about it?"

"Management only became concerned when they realized that thousands of doses of vaccine had been contaminated."

"How did that happen?"

"Technicians were not taking showers between working on the two different kinds of vaccine, so the adenoviruses they were using to make one vaccine was crossing over to contaminate the other vaccine. Finally, workers started placing yellow tags on all the contaminated batches."

"Did management know?"

"Of course they knew! But they were more concerned that the FDA was going to make an onsite inspection so they had workers remove the tags. Then they put them back on after the inspectors left."

"Wow, how many doses were involved?"

"That's difficult to say because you only test batches, not individual doses. But at the time they knew that at least 15 million dose equivalents had been contaminated and thrown away, presumably to hide the evidence. Now we know it was closer to 400 million."

"That's 400 million people that could have been vaccinated."

"Yup, all that vaccine squandered!"

"But it sounds like the chickens are finally coming home to roost."

"Indeed, it was all the result of jamming through Operation Warp Speed."

"Anything else?"

"Only that now the government can't afford to buy any more vaccines because they spent so much money purchasing vaccines against biological weapons for our Strategic Stockpile. And you know who got the lion's share of those contracts?

"BioSolutions?"

"Bingo!"

"Are you still working for them?"

"Nope, all of that happened before I quit. But I still have my correspondence with them."

"Keep it in case anything new comes out."

"Trust me, I will."

CHAPTER 11

Fire

Hermit's Peak, New Mexico
May 20, 2022

"A Barringa illena, corazon contento."
Juana Lopez, Las Vegas Red Cross Shelter

It was difficult to breath on May 20, 2022. The latest Covid variants were on the rise and the sun skulked behind a pallid blanket of hot dry air. Ericka had to use her windshield wipers to sweep the black embers off her rental car.

"So how should I describe this fire, Paulo?"

The head of the Environmental Institution at Northern Arizona University scratched his heavy beard.

"Ten years ago I would have said such a wind driven fire event was unprecedented. Today I'd have to say it is just part of the new world we are living in. But you could also say it was the result of a mistake."

"How so?"

"Someone picked the wrong day to start a fire."

"You mean someone was burning their brush?"

"Sort of, but he was working for the Santa Fe National Forest Service."

"Why was he burning anything?"

"Every year the National Forest Service tries to thin out any forests that have grown too dense and do a controlled burn."

"Does that make sense?"

"It is actually good policy, but our record breaking winds and dry conditions have made it very tricky to decide when to burn. The National Forest Service has apologized for their mistake."

"So you think this prolonged drought is unprecedented."

"Unprecedented, catastrophic, apocalyptic, worst drought in 1,200 years. You're the wordsmith, take your pick."

"And you think this drastic climate change has all happened in just the past ten years?"

"Of course, it has been building ever since the Industrial Revolution, but now we seem to have raced past several tipping points. It's estimated that by 2030, the world will be experiencing over 500 climate-related disasters every year."

"Oh great. That means I'll have to write two gloom and doom stories every day."

Ericka pulled into a shelter in the largest town in the region where an army of locals provided breakfast, lunch, and dinner for 200 people a day. Exhausted evacuees pulled up in cars and trucks with all their belongings and pet crates tied onto the roofs of their cars.

An old man walked into the shelter with a scrap of paper with three handwritten telephone numbers.

"Can you call my friend Garcia?"

"I'll see what I can do."

"Thank you, ma'am, they just took me from my home. I don't have a cell phone or place to go."

"I'm sorry. None of the numbers are in service."

"What am I going to do? I've had a tough time lately. My wife died a year ago. I have bad heart and I fell and broke two ribs a month ago."

"Don't worry sir. I'm sure they can take care of all that. You should go inside and have a nice hot meal. You know 'A barringa illena, corazon contento!'"

"Full belly, happy heart! How do you know Spanish?"

"I'm a writer. We get around."

"You're a very nice lady. I come from Rociada, the most beautiful place in the world. My ancestors settled there when it was still part of the Spanish Empire. It is nestled in the mountains and has lots of water. I want to go back but they won't let me."

"Did you lose your house?"

"No it was saved, but my barn and farm equipment was lost. I don't know what I'm going to do. I don't have any insurance. I just come down here every day to see if I can find my friend Garcia. I hope he is still alive."

CHAPTER 12

The Medic

Mariupol, Ukraine
May 21, 2022

Gregor groped for his cell phone ringing annoyingly beside his cot.

"Good morning sunshine!"

"Ugh, good morning, Petra. What time is it?"

"5 a.m."

"OK, where are we going today?"

"I can't tell you. But get your passport, press vest, and body armor."

"Sounds interesting! Who are we seeing?"

"Ukraine's newest hero."

"Who's that?"

"You'll find out. Oh, and bring your bathing suit since we may go for a swim."

"I don't have a bathing suit."

"Neither do I!"

As soon as they got out of Kyiv they drove south through the countryside that made Ukraine the place Russians all wanted to go for their holidays.

"Now can you tell me where we are going?"

"Mariupol."

"Mariupol?"

"Yes, my family used to drive down there every summer. We had a boat on the Black Sea."

"So we are going boating?"

"No, we are going to the steel plant in Avolstal."

"How can we get in?"

"I have some contacts. But you better put on your bulletproof jacket. We're going to meet a doctor called Taira."

"You mean the athlete who was going to go to the Invictus Games?"

"But she didn't go. As soon as the war broke out, she signed up to be a medic. I met her during our training."

"How did she wind up in Mariupol?"

"She's been there from the beginning. They offered to evacuate her, but she chose to stay until the bitter end."

Their military escort led them through the underground tunnels to a makeshift bunker where Petra saw Taira sitting on the floor. She looked exhausted, but still beautiful with short-cropped blond hair, aviator's glasses, and war-torn army fatigues.

"How are you, my brave friend?"

"Petra, so who is your boyfriend?"

"He is not my boyfriend Taira! This is Gregor McFadden. He writes for an American newspaper and wants to ask you some questions."

"Fire away!"

"I've heard a lot about you. What have you seen down here?"

"We've seen everything. We often don't have time to treat soldier's wounds, so we have to amputate their arms and legs. Sometimes we have to work in the dark."

"That shouldn't be a problem for you! Taira used to be famous for doing epidurals with her eyes closed."

"True, I taught myself to close my eyes and feel between the vertebrae for just the right entry point. It is actually more accurate than using your vision. I taught the other students to do the same. But most of them chicken out and open their eyes at the last minute. I always keep mine shut."

"Must come in handy down here."

"The worst cases are the children. Last week we had a young boy and his sister. They were both starving and had multiple injuries. I kept trying to calm down the poor boy, who was frightened and in deep pain.

We lost him after a long effort. He simply didn't have the strength to go on. I stood there crying uncontrollably, saying 'I hate this! I hate this!' until the next patient was carried in."

"Who was he?"

"A Russian soldier. He may have been the one who shot the young boy for all I know."

"What did you do?"

"I told our soldiers to treat him gently because he was a prisoner of war. Then I cared for him like anyone else.

But I'm afraid I must get back to work. Petra, do you need to powder your nose?"

Once they were inside the washroom Taira embraced her friend.

"I have slipped my tampon applicator into your left pocket. It has 256 gigabytes of video taken by my body cam. It shows everything we have been through. Can you see that it gets shown to the world?"

"Of course my dear friend. Are you sure you won't take the offer to evacuate?"

"No this is where I'm supposed to be. Just make sure your boyfriend gets the videotape out."

"For the last time. He's not my boyfriend Taira!"

"You were always a little oblivious Petra! Be well and have a good life."

After leaving the bunker, Gregor and Petra drove through 15 Russian checkpoints with Taira's tampon tucked away safely in Petra's purse. The ruse worked. The soldiers were embarrassed to inspect the tampon too closely.

That night Gregor e-mailed the video to the Boston Globe who sent it out over the Internet.

A week later Russian television reported that Taira had been arrested for distributing anti-Russian literature. She was clearly drugged and groggily read a prepared statement telling Ukrainians to lay down their arms because their situation was lost.

She was never seen again.

CHAPTER 13

Terror by Error?

Columbia University, New York City
May 25, 2022

"The list of coincidences is getting
verrrrry long."
Richard Ebright, Ph.D.
Rutgers University

Sylvia met Stan Kramer at the Columbia Faculty Club. Since the Globe was paying they both ordered salad and smoked salmon marinated in maple syrup.

"I can't believe you are calling for yet another look at the origins of Covid, Stan."

"Were you convinced by the CIA report?"

"Well, they did get rid of all the conspiracy theories, leaving the two most obvious choices- that the virus spilled over from nature like other zoonotic diseases or that it escaped from a lab.

But most of the epidemiologists I've spoken to say the idea that Covid came from a lab is bonkers."

"Epidemiologists are precisely the wrong people to ask. You see, their entire careers have been based on the idea that you can go out into the field and track zoonotic diseases to their reservoir species. So they build their little silos and don't bother to step outside."

"Then who do you ask?"

"There are just as many well-qualified scientists who are versed in biological warfare and techniques used to insert amino acids into viruses to make them more virulent. They think it is highly improbable such a potent virus just happened to pop up outside the very lab that was doing that kind of research."

"Who are some of those scientists?"

"Michael Osterholm, head of Minnesota's Public Health Department, Stephen Lipschitz at Harvard, Allison Graham at Yale, Alina Chan at MIT, Richard Ebright at Rutgers and my co-author Ned Nelson here at Columbia. They all think that the kind of research being done in places like Wuhan and here at the University of South Carolina should be banned."

"There are also some prominent science writers who favor the lab leak hypothesis."

"Yes from the New York Times, MIT's Technology Review and the Bulletin of Atomic Scientists."

"And you agree?"

"Ned and I think the CIA didn't go deep enough in their 12-page report. They essentially copped out saying they couldn't get enough information from China. But we think the data that would settle the issue is in the gene sequences of the virus and notes from the U.S. labs and agencies that funded the research here and in China."

"Which labs and agencies?"

"The NIH, the Defense Department, the University of South Carolina, and Enviro-Wellness down in Jersey."

"What were they doing?"

"They were perfecting ways of inserting sequences of amino acids into the virus genomes and funding Chinese scientists to do that in Wuhan."

"Who was doing that in this country?"

"Dr. Burroughs down in Charleston applied for a grant to insert a sequence of eight amino acids from human lung tissue into bat viruses to make it easier for the viruses to attach to epithelium cells in human lungs and airways."

"In other words to make them more infectious. "

"Correct."

"Damn!"

"And Enviro-Wellness was funded to collect the viruses from bats and work with Chinese scientists to reverse-engineer the viruses to make them more virulent, causing a more severe illness. The intent of the work was to prevent emerging pathological threats, but it could have also created a more clinically dangerous illness."

"In other words, Covid-19?"

"Right!"

"The researchers who know about this research have remained largely silent because of peer pressure. Some were just too busy trying to saves lives, others lost their jobs or had to change their names because of academic politics."

"But you've changed your mind on this as well, haven't you?"

"Yes, I was originally chair of the commission set up by Modern Medicine Magazine to investigate the origins of Covid. We appointed Donald Warshall to lead the task force but found out he had engineered a public statement in the magazine that said any hypothesis that Covid could have leaked from a lab was a conspiracy theory."

"Not very scientific."

"For sure. I finally disbanded the task force because I had concerns that several of the members of the commission had conflicts of interest because of their ties to the Enviro-Wellness group."

"And I understand you have also grown disillusioned with NIH."

"Yes, there has been a constant drip of unsettling information that has cast an ever-darkening cloud over the agency.

They simply insist that Covid could not have resulted from work they sponsored, but their blanket denials are no longer good enough."

"Do you think there is a cover-up?"

"Well, several researchers removed the most crucial sequences from their labs and computers."

"And that could have been the smoking gun."

"Yes, they would have made it clear that the U.S. was just as culpable as the researcher in Wuhan or the lab ferret that sneezed on him!"

"And now 20 million people may have died from an everyday accident on research done to make a more virulent virus."

"If the truth comes out, we would either look like international pariahs, or fools with egg on our face!"

"Thanks, Stan. I think I have my story."

CHAPTER 14

A Sea of Icebergs

Svalbard, Norway
May 28, 2022

A sea of icebergs floated below Ericka as she photographed them through the window of her flight to Norway. They had broken off the snow-covered expanse of Greenland and were doomed to die in the grip of the warming Atlantic Ocean. After flying over Snufaloss volcano in Iceland, they cruised into the Svalbard airport.

Jake Kerowak met her at the gate.

"Welcome to the northernmost town on the planet, home to more polar bears than people."

"Thank you so much for calling me, Jake."

"You know I always think of you when I have another adventure. How are you doing?"

"Same as always, chronicling the end of our planet!"

"But always so full of optimism, despite your miserable task."

"You know me, can't resist a good story. And the end of the world is a pretty good story if you're a mordant science writer."

"You also can't resist a good adventure."

"Got that right. When do we get started, tomorrow?"

"It's all the same, remember, 24 hours of daylight. Just stow your camera in my snowmobile beside my rifle. We can get you settled in my place later."

"You think of everything Jake."

"Try to."

As they approached Jake's research area, Ericka spotted polar bears ambling out of the hills heading down to Svalbard Bay.

"They seem a lot more friendly than last time."

"They are. Normally they would be spread out on the ice

defending their seal-hunting territories. But since the ice has melted they have been forced to live on land."

"I would think they would be more territorial with only limited resources."

"Usually, they would be. But not this year, the melting ice has given them a present."

"What's that?"

"Look over there where the bears are heading."

"My God, one is standing on the carcass of a whale! How did it die?"

"We don't know but we figure she has been under the ice for at least a year. Bears were feeding on the same half-frozen carcass last summer."

"So, they are at a big banquet of rotting flesh. No wonder they are so happy."

"Yup we figure that there are still over 3 billion calories of meat on the whale carcass. At least 80 bears have traveled over fifty miles to get here."

"Can we get closer?"

"We can do one better. Help me unpack this drone."

Jake attached the rotors and as they whirled into motion Ericka thought of Gregor. She felt guilty that she was safely ensconced in Norway while he pursued his suicidal mission in Ukraine.

A bear raised his blood-stained snout as the drone buzzed over his massive head, others had torn a large hole out of the frozen side of the carcass.

Ericka's thoughts about Gregor faded over dinner with Jake.

"Try this, it's hakarl, the specialty of the house."

"Ack it tastes like horse piss!"

"Close! Here have some Akvavit quick."

"What was that?"

"Greenland shark. Icelanders soak it in urine and then bury it in the sand for a year. It's really just an excuse to get snookered on Akvavit."

"I don't need such an excuse, thank you very much!"

"Well, you know Icelanders. They'll do anything for a little fun."

"Tell me more about these Greenland sharks. I understand they grow very old."

"Yup, up to 400 years. Their metabolism is very slow but they can lunge after large seals and they can even catch large fish. They just open their huge mouths and suction does the rest.

We have even found whole caribou and polar bear in their gullets. They may catch them when they are swimming between floes of ice but they probably scavenge them off the sea floor after they have been wounded by another bear or shot and drowned."

"I would love to see one."

"We might just be able to arrange that. We have seen one prowling around the carcass of the whale. I have a dry suit that should fit you."

The following day, Jake and Ericka donned their gear and once in the water, they caught up with a 15-foot shark swimming in slow circles around the whale carcass. She was placid and looked a little goofy with her ever-grinning mouth. Ericka had to swim hard to catch up until the shark heard the bubbles rising from her SCUBA tank. Although sharks usually flee at the sound of bubbles, this one turned and eyed Ericka with intent curiosity.

Ericka remembered Jake's warning that Greenland sharks catch their prey by simply opening their huge mouths so she quickly clambered up the slippery flank of the half-submerged carcass.

"That was exhilarating!"

"Glad you enjoyed it. We'll skip the hakarl tonight."

CHAPTER 15

"The Way"

Saint Paul-les-Durance, France
June 1, 2022

"I would like to see nuclear fusion become a practical power source. It would provide an inexhaustible supply of energy, without pollution or global warming. It is the scientific discovery I would most like to see in my lifetime."
Stephen Hawking, Ph.D.
Time Magazine 2010

"Impressive discipline," said Gregor to Petra as the unit they were embedded in gradually retreated through the streets of Severodonetsk.

As the soldiers in the rear provided cover, the soldiers in front fell back behind them to set up new positions.

"Block by block they are leaving the city but all the while they are picking off the new Russian conscripts that are being forced to advance."

"You would think Russia would remember its own history when the Czar's soldiers retreated, and Napoleon's army followed until it had outrun its supply lines. Starvation and winter did the rest."

"You would think so. But our unit is just retreating to better positions in Lysychansk. Petrovich says they will dig in there and use the advantage of their hilltop position to inflict further damage on the Russian invaders."

"Hope it works."

"Why Gregor, what happened to your objectivity?"

"Gone with the wind. I can't take any more of this war. I have seen too many dying kids and maimed bodies."

"But you have to keep telling our story."

"I'm not sure I'm up to it anymore. I need a rest from all this mayhem. Besides my stories are slipping off the front page as my country continues to be convulsed with mass shootings, surging Covid cases and out-of-control forest fires."

"What will you do?"

"I'm thinking of slipping back into southern France to cover what could be the biggest story of our lifetime."

"What's that?"

"Nuclear fusion. Do you want to come? I should be able to get the Globe to hire you as my full-time translator."

"But I speak French like a Spanish cow."

"Tres idiomatique! You're hired."

Two weeks later Petra and Gregor were driving through the lavender fields and vineyards of Provence on their way to Saint Paul-les-Durance.

Gregor read their travel brochure.

"Saint Paul-les-Durance used to be where they floated logs down from the calcareous cliffs of the tree-lined Gorge du Verdon.

Now the village of only 1,000 people is going to be home to La Centre du Atom in the most expensive building ever built."

The director met them at the gate.

"Bonjour, je suis Claude Lambin. Welcome to The International Thermonuclear Experimental Reactor."

"ITER?"

"Oui, it means 'The Way' in Latin."

"Fitting."

"Bien sur. We feel this is the way to solve the most probleme serieux ever faced by mankind."

"You mean humankind!"

"Ah oui, pardon Madame! We hope to prove that fusion can be used to provide a limitless supply of energy without carbon emissions in the next 30 years."

"Haven't engineers been saying nuclear fusion was 30 years off since the 1920s?"

"Mais oui, because they were only investing a measly ten million dollars a year. Now countries and billionaires are putting big money into fusion research."

"How do you plan to do it?"

"Down there we are building our own Tokamak.

"It looks like something out of Star Wars!"

"The first one was built by the Soviet Union."

"Russians again. I thought I could escape them."

"Here at ITER we welcome Russia. Her scientists were the first to be able to generate plasmas hot enough so fusion could happen.

She is still one of our main funders. In fact, we are waiting for them to deliver a magnet for the top of our Tokamak. It sits in St. Petersburg waiting to be shipped. So far Russia's involvement with us hasn't changed in any way."

"So, it's like the cooperation between Russia and the United States for the International Space Station until that became politicized."

"Yes, we hope to stay under the radar so we can continue to be a project for peace."

"That may be no small feat."

"All of the 35 countries who are part of this project are fully aware that dropping the ball could easily mean the demise of the entire project. They realize it is a huge global responsibility."

"In other words, if politicians can just hold the planet together for another 30 years, scientists should be able to solve the energy problem."

"We like to think so. There are already 150 Tokamaks in the world. They are mostly in universities and research facilities. If all of them could be retrofitted to produce electricity commercially, our global energy problem would be largely solved."

That evening Gregor and Petra discussed their day over two large platters of fruits de mer and a carafe of Villa Beaulieu de Cassis.

"I will have to tell Ericka about "The Way". I saw my first Tokamak with her at the Swiss Plasma Center in Lausanne.

"Tell me about this Ericka."

"Nothing to tell really. She broke my heart. I'm still trying to recover."

"I would like to help if you will let me."

"Always the healer, aren't you?"

"I suppose."

"I would like that very much."

CHAPTER 16

Half-assed Gasification

Kansas
June 5, 2022

Ericka sat on the edge of a cornfield, watching workers pile bales of corn stalks into a large tank in the back of a large white semi-trailer. The chief scientist of a new start-up company stood beside her.

"Tell me how this all came about, Shane."

"Well, in 2020 I had a modest idea. Instead of gasifying biomass at high temperatures to produce hydrogen, why not just cook it at low temperatures to produce an oil, which can be pumped underground to be sequestered for millions of years? Steinhard calls my idea 'half-assed gasification.'"

"Who's Steinhard?"

"My partner."

"And companies are willing to pay you to do this?"

"Yes, Steinhard has lined up companies like Microsoft, Shopify, and Stripe to pay us $600 a ton to offset their emissions.

"That's the same price Climate Works is charging to suck carbon dioxide out of the air in Iceland."

"Not a coincidence! You see the beauty of our system is that it's simple. We don't have to raise large amounts of money and build huge air-sucking machines.

"Yes, their process reminds me of the Morlocks in the Time Machine by H. G. Wells."

"Never saw it."

"It takes place in a dystopic future that is so polluted that humanity has evolved into two separate species, the pastoral Elios who look like they come from Southern California and live an idyllic life on the surface, and the Morlocks who slave underground running vast machines that suck oxygen into their underground lairs. They only come out at night to prey on the Elios."

"I always thought of us as David fighting Goliath. We have already locked away 5,500 tons of carbon. Climate Works has only sequestered 4,000 tons."

"But that's all just a drop in the bucket."

"For sure. Someone will have to build half a million Climate Works' ORCA-style sucking machines to remove society's annual rate of carbon emissions. We think we can do it far more efficiently by using leftover plant material from farms and trees thinned to prevent forest fires. We make them into biochar fertilizer to go back into the soil and our bio-oil to be sequestered in empty oil wells."

"Won't you be competing with the ethanol industry?"

"No, they only use the kernels of corn to make ethanol. We use the husks left over from growing that corn."

"Their problem is they are using food to make fuel and are planning to use a pipeline to pump their waste carbon to far-away wells."

"I don't like making fuel from food and the public doesn't like pipelines."

"Pipelines are actually the safest way to transport oil but that's their problem. We have a fleet of these trucks that can go from field to field, gasify the farm wastes and then deliver the oil to wells so it can be sequestered. We think we can eventually do the whole process for about $60 a ton."

"So you have a head start, but how will you fare as the market develops? The next generation of carbon capturing farms is supposed to remove a million tons of carbon a year."

"They are part of the whole 'we can build our way out of the environmental crisis' mindset. We think there will always be a niche market for our low-cost method. The way to survive is to think small and think smart."

"But will corporations continue to buy up enough carbon removal credits to support your work?"

"We are betting that governments will see they have to step in and subsidize all these different practices so the economy can create multiple carbon removal markets."

"So you're saying we can't put our hope in these pie-in-the-sky projections that we can have unlimited supplies of clean energy so we can continue to live as unsustainably as we have in the past."

"Yes, we have to learn to live within our means. Otherwise, we will be trapped in this world of climate chaos with no way to recover."

"Grim thought."

"But a spur for us to not bury our head in the sand or pursue grandiose expensive solutions when smaller simpler ones can ultimately be more effective."

CHAPTER 17

Sylvia's Mystery

Cambridge, Massachusetts
June 6, 2022

Sylvia pulled her rowing shell off the rack of the Cambridge Boat House. Rowing always helped her clear her head to shape her stories and ponder mysteries for new ones.

Today's Covid mystery involved scores of Instagrams she had received from friends showing the results of their at-home Covid tests. Why were so many of her close friends suddenly getting sick when before it was mostly just people you read about?

Was the virus spreading much faster than was being reported? Were her friends, normally careful people, starting to do riskier things?

And why was she feeling so darn lousy? By the time she finished her row, she knew what she would do.

"Hi, Dr. Della Bovi? This is Sylvia Grenfeld. Can I get some help with a personal problem?"

"Of course, free consults are one of the perks of being a health writer, but only if you call me Gina."

"Thanks, Gina. Last week my daughter Sondra came home from school complaining of a sore throat and chills. That night she had a hundred-degree temperature and I resigned myself to the fact that our whole family was finally going to get Covid after all our months of being so careful."

"And now you have it?"

"I don't know. I have this scratchy throat and my Lauren Bacall whiskey voice, but I have tested negative twice."

"Three times is a charm."

"Don't say that!"

"My husband never developed symptoms or tested positive but both kids have coughs, runny noses, and are always tired."

"Those symptoms could be from all kinds of things-colds or allergies exacerbated by being run down at the end of a long stressful school year."

"Yes, I've racked my brain for what it could be. We have been wearing masks so long we may have lost immunity to fight off all those bugs kids bring home to us at the beginning of school."

"Or it could be Covid-19"

"But I haven't tested positive."

"Have you been fully boosted and vaccinated?"

"That's like asking the Pope if he's Catholic."

"The reason I ask is that if you are vaccinated your immune system seems to kick in much faster than if you aren't vaccinated."

"So?"

"It changes everything that happens next."

"In what way?"

"It slows down how quickly the virus can reproduce so you were less likely to test positive after you were exposed to your daughter."

"But why do I still feel lousy?"

"Even though you didn't have enough virions in your body to test positive, you may still have had enough to trigger your immune system."

"So, my symptoms were because of my immune response, not because of the viruses themselves."

"Bingo!"

"Couldn't my editor say this is all just anecdotal evidence?"

"He could but tell him the plural of anecdote is data!"

"But why does my husband feel just fine?"

"Probably because his immune system fought off the virus."

"The kids all got sick, he didn't get sick at all and I got half sick. It just doesn't seem very fair."

"Viruses aren't known for their fairness."

"I dunno, perhaps I was just too busy to get really sick."

"That would just be another one of those women's dilemmas we often find ourselves in."

"Now there is a story you could write about."

"Unlikely, remember my editor is a man."

"Backward creatures, aren't they?"

"Yeah, but kind of nice to sleep with."

"Glad you still have your sense of humor, Sylvia. Good to see you, get some sleep, take care of yourself and stay well."

CHAPTER 18

The Game Changer?

Snohomish County, Washington
June 9, 2022

Ericka liked the boyish-looking CEO of Antares Energy but wasn't going to be taken in by some green washing snow job.

"What's with the black sneakers and magenta shoelaces?"

"Oh, these? Magenta is the fundamental color of nuclear fusion. When fusion occurs the plasma glows hot pink."

"And you think nuclear fusion is the energy of the future."

"No doubt about it."

"So, how did you get into the field?"

"I used to do a lot of mountain climbing. The views from Mount Rainier were spectacular, but year after year the amount of snow and glaciers dwindled."

"And…?"

"Well, when I went to college, I wanted to do something to change the trajectory we were on and thought fusion was the best way to do it. But after four years of study, I concluded that nuclear fusion would never happen in my lifetime, so I switched and got my PhD in aerospace engineering instead. I figured I might work for Boeing just down the road from here."

"Then what happened to change your mind?"

"Technology. Major advances were made in everything from supercomputers to fiber optics. All of a sudden you had nuclear fusion breakthroughs in places like MIT, Cavendish, China, and ITER in France."

"Yes, my colleague just did a story about ITER. He thinks they will win the race to produce commercial energy."

"What, with sixty-year-old technology, government funding

and Russia as a partner? In this day and age their partnership could fall apart at any time. We have billionaires like Bill Gates and Jeff Bezos behind us."

"Oh, and why not Musk?"

"Oh, he's far too busy tweeting and preparing to fly off to Mars."

"But seriously, what do you think gives you the advantage?"

"Technology again. Some people have shown that you can produce a lot of energy with fusion, and others have shown you can do fusion reactions. But no one has made electricity yet. In just a few short years we will be able to produce electricity directly from fusion at about one cent per kilowatt hour."

"Too cheap to meter. Haven't we heard that before?"

"Yes, that was an unfortunate promise made by the nuclear industry in the bad old fission days."

"But what makes you think you won't come up against similar unforeseen circumstances?"

"Oh we will, but I think with sufficient funding we will solve each problem and be able to unleash the power of the sun right here on earth."

"But exactly how do you plan to do that?"

"In June we were the first private company to heat fusion plasma to over 100 million degrees Fahrenheit, which is the ideal temperature needed to fuse atoms of hydrogen into helium. Now our Trenta plant is producing fusion reactions every morning at 3 am.

But instead of using fusion energy to heat water and run a steam turbine, our plant will move the plasma back and forth through a circular magnet to make electricity directly."

"Interesting. But how much fuel will you need?"

"We use an isotope of hydrogen called deuterium. See this Coke bottle? It takes this volume of deuterium to replace a million gallons of oil and power over 800 homes for a year. The ocean contains enough deuterium to generate billions of years of carbon-free energy."

"So you could use it to power the grid."

"Yes, but we're not focusing on making big power plants. We want to make 50-megawatt systems that we can put on a truck and then ship and install on site to power something like a data center. Our next step is to mass produce the systems and distribute them as fast as possible to help stop future climate change.

We will be manufacturing them in this former aerospace facility. I had them remove the doors and put in these large windows so we can see the soaring flanks of Mount Baker and the North Cascade Range.

I've watched the climate change in those mountains ever since I moved to Washington. They are a towering symbol of what is at stake here. What we're trying to do is a big challenge, but it is definitely worth it. The world needs this technology."

"You know you have almost convinced me. I see my unfortunate role as being a skeptic and chronicler of the rapid decline of our planet, but you have given me hope that if we can just muddle through the next thirty years or so, you, or someone like you, may just solve this fusion conundrum. And that could be exactly the game changer we need."

"Glad I made a believer out of you."

"Easy there, don't go that far. This isn't my first rodeo you know. You still have a long way to go."

"I know but we think we are on our way and will get there first."

"I'll be the first one to congratulate you when you do. Good luck!"

CHAPTER 19

The Danger Season

Yellowstone National Park
Gardiner, Montana
June 14, 2022

Ericka pulled up to the Northern Entrance to Yellowstone National Park. She wanted to see the geysers, steaming pools, wolves, bear and elk that she had read so much about as a young girl.

"Good morning, I'm from the Boston Globe. I'm here to cover the effects of the heat dome."

"I'm sorry Ma'am. We've just received orders to lock the gate. All five entrances to the park are being closed."

"Because of the rain?"

"Because of everything. It started last winter when we got 400% more snow than usual. Now the unseasonably higher temperatures have melted the snow and the water is rushing down off the Beartooth and Absaroka Mountains.

Top that with the four or five inches of rain we had last night and you have a real disaster. This morning the Yellowstone River crested 10 feet above normal at the convergence of the north and south forks. The raging waters have caused rockslides and washed out numerous bridges. We expect several houses to topple into the Yellowstone later today."

"Can I get in to see some of the damage?"

"I'm sorry I can't let you in, but there's a helicopter company in Bozeman that has been evacuating some of the campsites. They might be able to help you."

After spending the night in the only motel still open in Bozeman, Ericka was able to charter a helicopter and fly out with a former ranger who took an instant shine to her.

"This here's the Yellowstone River."

"Holy shit, it has washed out the highway in four or five places."

"Yup at each turn it has undermined the highway."

"How long will it take to repair it?"

"I'm not sure it makes much sense to repair it. We might have to just abandon the highway and build another one inland."

Further up the river they saw the river engulfing a house. It tore off the house's porches and garage before tossing the entire structure into the river where it bobbed downstream. It finally lodged in a giant pile of trees and lumber under a bridge that was groaning and buckling in the rushing waters.

"Has anyone been killed or injured?"

"Not so far as we know."

"Why do you think this park is getting so much attention when millions of people are starving to death and dying from heatstroke in places like India?"

"I think it's because Yellowstone is America's most iconic national park. The environmental writer Wallace Stegner said that the national parks are America's greatest idea."

"For me, the reason this makes such a compelling story is that it shows how dangerous the world has become. Every summer we can expect to see more heat waves, fires, flooding, and storms."

————

Two days later Ericka was pounding out her copy under a sweltering blob of hot air centered over St. Louis.

"The heat dome is swelling and contracting back and forth across the country like a giant amoeba placing over a hundred million human beings under a heat wave advisory.

The curved squall line spreading out like a bow wave along the northern edge of the expanding heat dome is expected to be the center of the most intense area of thunderstorm propagation.

Forecasters are warning three-digit temperatures could spawn tornadoes, hail and lines of damaging derecho storms."

She headlined her story "The Danger Season," before throwing it in the trash and starting over again.

CHAPTER 20

Ghost Ships and Soft Gold

Shanghai, China
June 17, 2022

Sylvia always felt the best way to see any new city was from a boat. It was especially enticing after Shanghai's two-month long lockdown. Twenty-five million people wanted to get out, see friends, and breathe some fresh air.

She walked through the tall modern buildings of Pudong to the Shanghai Ferry Company that ran ferries back and forth across the Huangpu River. After boarding, she made her way to the bridge where Captain Liu had invited her for a glass of Shaoxing wine.

"You are allowed to drink when you are working?"

"Oh, I'm not going to drink, you are. It's against the rules but we Shanghai residents have always been a bit of a thorn in the side of the Beijing authorities."

"How so?"

"See those colonial buildings over there? Beijing has nothing like that. They were built by British merchants after the Opium Wars."

"I've never quite understood the Opium Wars."

"Well, the British were angry because we had tea, silk and porcelain, and they didn't have anything we wanted to buy. So they started shipping poppies from their Indian colonies to get us hooked on opium so they would have something to sell us.

Our celestial leader confiscated fourteen hundred tons of their opium, to protect us, but the British used that as a red flag to start the war. It was a humiliating defeat for China, but it opened up Shanghai to the West whose merchants built all those beautiful buildings over there on the Bund."

"Why it's beautiful. What's that Victorian building with the green glowing light tower?"

"It used to be the Cathay Hotel. The authorities renamed it the Peace Hotel because in its day it was the epitome of colonialism, greed and capitalism."

"Sounds interesting. Who built it?"

"Victor Sassoon. He was the second baronet of Bombay. He came from a banking family in Damascus who set up shop in Shanghai in the 1920's."

"And I thought he sold hair products."

"Wrong Sassoon!

This one was a capitalist dog, but he invested millions of dollars in Shanghai. Most of the beautiful old buildings that make up our skyline were built and financed by him. They are what makes Beijing feel so inferior."

"Can't you get in trouble for saying such things?"

"As I was saying, he was the worst sort of running dog playboy capitalist pig, who hung out with whores, drunks and movie stars."

"Are you sure you haven't been having a few nips behind my back? But I am here to have you tell me about what happened to you back in 2019."

"It was a hot summer night and just as I was pulling into the Bund for the last trip of my day, an American container ship pulled out on her way back to your Long Beach in California."

"Know it well."

"Her crew was maneuvering it very carefully. You know this is the busiest port in the world?"

"Didn't know that."

"I was watching another large ship that was also steaming up the channel but suddenly, blip, it disappeared off my GPS screen. But a few minutes later my screen showed it back on the dock, then back in the channel, then back on the dock, before it disappeared for good.

I picked up my binoculars and went out on deck to scrutinize the waterfront. There was the ship lying in her berth. She had been there the whole time."

"Incredible!"

"Hundreds of other captains have reported similar experiences. On one occasion a container ship slammed into the Bund scattering pedestrians in all directions."

"Hmm, years ago I was aboard an oceanographic vessel and suddenly we found ourselves in the middle of a midnight naval operation. We hadn't picked up the signals of any of the ships on our radar. Their commanding officer radioed us to leave the area because they were doing secret maneuvers for a covert mission. Never knew what that was all about."

"And I've heard Russia jammed the Ukrainian GPS systems when they attacked Crimea, and that Russian mobile electronic warfare units disrupt GPS systems during Putin's public appearances."

"But why would someone jam GPS signals here in Shanghai?"

"Some people think it is a secret government plot."

"But what do you think?"

"I think it's sand pirates. We have hundreds of them."

"Sand pirates? What do they do?"

"At night they lower huge pipes to the bottom of the Yangtze River and suck up tons of sand illegally. They can make $80,000 for a few hours work. We call it 'soft gold.'"

"What happens to the sand?"

"See all those ugly buildings on the new side of the river? All made out of cement made with sand, most of it illegal."

"Can't the authorities arrest them?"

"That's where GPS jamming comes in. The sand pirates have figured out a way to spoof the GPS signals of all the boat traffic in Shanghai."

"How do you know this?"

"My father was a sound engineer before the Cultural Revolution when we were shipped off to be re-educated. They had us sing, dance, rat on our neighbors, and learn communist songs. We called it 'Commie Camp'."

"Why I went to a commie camp as well. But it was in Pough-keepsie, New York! I'm what we like to call a red diaper baby. Grew up reading the Workers Weekly in Flatbush."

"You must tell me more about your commie camp over some more Shaoxing wine. Can you meet me at the Yu Garden teahouse tonight at 7:00? I have someone you should meet."

CHAPTER 21

"Water Always Wins"

Yu Garden
Shanghai, China
July 18, 2022

"We must make friends with flooding."
Yu Kongjian
As quoted by Ericka Geis
MIT Technology Review
December 21, 2021

"Good morning, Sylvia. How do you like our Exquisite Jade Rock?"

"Why Mr. Liu, it's huge! How did it get here?"

"Pirates."

"Again?"

"Yes it was being transported down the Huangpu River on its way to being placed in front of the Imperial Palace in Beijing."

"When was that?"

"Back in about 1100 AD, but rumor has it that pirates sank the boat and the 5-ton boulder sat on the bottom until it was salvaged and made the centerpiece of our Garden of Happiness in 1559. It's another reason Beijing is jealous of us."

They strolled past giant koi swimming lazily through tranquil ponds under bridges, moon gates and carved dragons that adorned them. Soon they were in front of the lacquered walls of Huxingting Tea House.

"How old is this building?"

"Remember the Opium Wars?"

"How could I forget?"

"The British used this tea house as their base of operations in

1842, and the Japanese soldiers desecrated it in 1942. Afterwards, it was repaired by one of our local heroes Lianshun Han.

We nicknamed him Rockery Han for his artistry at creating these cranny-filled rock walls that mimic the water filled gorges of Central China. But I want you to meet our modern equivalent of Rockery Han, who instead of loving rocks, is a friend of flooding."

As if on cue, a dapper gentleman with shrewd eyes and a touch of gray hair emerged from the other side of the Exquisite Jade Rock.

"Sylvia I'd like to meet my old friend Yu Kongjian. We met as boys during the Cultural Revolution. He can tell you all about rockeries and water."

"Ni Hao Sylvia. Yes, we Chinese people have a long tradition of collecting interesting rock specimens and placing them in our homes to make miniature landscapes."

"Why, I remember seeing them at the Museum of Fine Arts in Boston."

"You mean the MFA."

"How do you know the MFA?"

"I visited it often when I was studying at the Design School."

"You were at Harvard?"

"Yes, that's why so many of my countrymen think I am an American spy."

"No Kongjian, it is because you don't like dams. They are considered to be symbols of power and progress by the authorities."

"But they are beginning to see the light."

"Kongjian has designed 30 'sponge cities' that retain up to 70% of their rainfall. Beijing's goal is to have a hundred such cities by 2030. That will affect over a million people."

"Very impressive. But tell me about your experiences during the Cultural Revolution."

"I hated it, but Kongjian loved it."

"Yes, I lived on a communal farm in Zhejian Province during the Mao years. I spent all day observing peasant wisdom. You see, for thousands of years Chinese farmers would build small ponds and berms so rainfall would infiltrate the soil and be saved for dry days. I watched the creek next to our village swell and retreat with the seasons."

"We are also having terrible flooding back at home in the United States."

"But you see, for me floods were a time of great excitement because fish come onto the fields and into ponds. But as China urbanized, we abandoned that knowledge in favor of your Western path. Now we must regain that knowledge and become friends with flooding once again."

"You can see one of Kongjian's projects over at Houtan Park."

"Yes, we built it on the site of an old steel mill located on a curve of the Huangpu River. We transformed the area for the 2010 Green Expo but our objective was not just to help create an unforgettable event, but to build a permanent public park as well.

A linear wetland runs through the center of the park that is used to treat polluted water from the Huangpu River. It has cascades and terraces that oxygenate the water while creating soothing water features. The water was used throughout the Expo for non-potable uses. The whole project was half a million dollars cheaper than a conventional water treatment plant."

"Impressive."

"Yes, but we try to do several things at once with our projects, so the wetland also acts as a sponge to hold water during floods."

"Like what you saw as a young boy in Zhejiang."

"Exactly! But what I like best are the terraces that both protect against flooding and are also reminiscent of Shanghai's agricultural heritage. Agricultural fields sit on the terraces. In the spring they are covered with miles of brilliant red poppies and blossom with golden sunflowers in summer. In the fall you can smell the ripening rice, and then enjoy the green color of clover all winter. It is a wonderful way for children learn about their agricultural past right here in the city."

"I wish we would do more of this kind of thing at home."

"You are starting to do it in places like New Orleans and on the fringes of New York City. But cities are just part of the entire landscape. You have to restore space for water to expand in upstream floodplains so the water level will be lower by the time it reaches the downstream cities. This is what we are starting to do in China."

"Sometimes I wish we could initiate things to clean up the environment as quickly as you do in China. How do you do it?"

Mr. Liu chimed in. "Much of it has to do with our heritage. Since Confucian times we have always had a large agricultural population ruled by highly trained bureaucrats that made decisions based on technology. We believe that our bureaucrats can make decisions that will be good for all our people in the long run.

For instance, when we decided it made more environmental sense to transport people around the country on trains instead of planes, it only took us ten years to make the transformation."

"And we are still stuck with poor staggering Amtrak! But what about your Covid lockdown and single child policy?"

"At the time the single child policy made a lot of sense. It helped lift us out of our cycle of famines and starvation and helped lead to urbanization. It was also one of the most effective population controls ever enacted."

"But it was so coercive."

"But hasn't your Supreme Court just forced women to have unwanted children, and said that Congress, not scientists and civil servants should regulate carbon emissions?"

"Yes, our Congress is not particularly known for its long term thinking."

"And you scorn the advice of your scientists and policy makers. We still admire our dedicated government workers. Why this garden even came about because Pan Yunduan failed his exam to become an imperial bureaucrat during the Ming dynasty, so he started building this garden instead."

"Hopefully things will change for us when enough liberal Supreme Court judges are appointed again."

"But you will still have your checks and balances to block making good decisions."

"Or prevent us from making bad ones. "

"But wouldn't it be better to have experts make such decisions?"

"Not if you believe in democracy. But you have given me food for thought. It is people like you who give me some hope for the future."

CHAPTER 22

Jamaica Bay, NY
July 5, 2022

Ericka composed a quick e-mail to Finbar.

"Hey Muldoon, Sylvia's story about Shanghai got me thinking. I'd like to write about the new islands that New York is building in Jamaica Bay."

"Just as long as I don't have to pay for another Jamaican vacation."

"Nope, that pitch comes in March."

"Will you fly down to New York?"

"No I'm feeling guilty about flying so much. A friend offered to drive me down in her Tesla."

She has solar shingles on her roof and a Tesla battery in her basement. About a third of the energy the system produces goes to heating and cooling her house, a third goes to running her car and a third goes back to the town's electrical grid. I might work the trip into my story or write a separate piece."

"What's come over you Ericka? You usually hit me up to fly you to some exotic location."

"I think it's important to think globally and write locally."

"OK, what is your angle, Ericka?"

"Well, it is my brother Ben's birthday. He lives on a houseboat just south of where they are building the new islands."

"Always an angle Ericka, always an angle. This better be good."

"Oh, it will be."

"Enjoy your trip."

Three days later Ericka was in the heart of New York City's surfing culture. A lot of it seemed to center around her brother's bar in Brooklyn. Kids would strap surfboards to the rafters of the bar, and when the surf was up they would grab their boards, jump on the subway and head to the Rockaways for a day of surfing.

Ericka stayed in one of Ben's rental houseboats. She awoke to the raucous calls of laughing gulls and stepped outside to see diamondback terrapins courting on the surface of the sunlit waters.

Overhead planes flew out of JFK Airport as they sped across Jamaica Bay in Ben's Boston Whaler. In short order they reached Broad Channel, a compact neighborhood that sits between Brooklyn and Queens. But its cluster of two story homes with docks for storing kayaks and outboards made it look more like a New England fishing village than a New York City borough.

Don Martin met Ben and Ericka at his dock and invited them inside.

"This is my humble abode. It's simple but has this spectacular view of the City all while sitting right here in the middle of one of the most important wildlife refuges on the East Coast. Over three hundred species of birds use the Jamaica Bay Refuge to stock up on food during their annual migrations."

"Amazing, but how did you get involved with cleaning up the bay?"

"My love affair started early. While the other kids headed off to play baseball after school, I'd take my kayak and explore the bay's labyrinths of creeks and marshes. I'd observe egrets and herons while catching striped bass and bluefish below flocks of diving terns. It wasn't like I was in the City at all. I had the place to myself.

Then during the Nineties, I started noticing changes. The water was getting rust-colored, and the salt marshes just seemed to be melting away. All that would be left in their wake were acre upon acre of lifeless mud flats with piles of dead bait fish rotting in the sun."

"What did you do about it?"

"Me and a handful of neighbors started bellyaching to state officials, but they just brushed us off saying we were just a bunch of blue collar guys who didn't know what we were talking about.

But we finally convinced them to do their own study and the DEC discovered that Jamaica Bay was losing about 50 acres of wetlands every year."

"That's the state's Department of Environmental Conservation?"

"Yup, they found that nitrogen coming out of four treatment plants that discharge wastewater into the Bay were killing off the marshes and fish. That was all we needed. We organized the Jamaica Bay EcoWatchers group and joined forces with the Natural Defense Council to sue the state."

"And it worked?"

"Yes, we won a hundred-million-dollar settlement that forced the Bloomberg Administration to upgrade their water treatment plants. It worked even better than we anticipated. The water is cleaner than I thought I'd ever see in my lifetime.

But we also received $15 million to build up the existing barrier beaches and add new marsh islands."

"How well do you think they will work?"

"If we had had them before Hurricane Sandy, a lot of the local houses wouldn't have washed away."

"Who's doing the work?"

"The Army Corps of Engineers. They have already added 160 acres and plan to restore 206 more acres on 5 new islands."

"Interesting that in China the decision to do these sorts of things comes from the top down but here we have to litigate from the bottom up to get anything done. But you must be very proud."

"We are, but we also know it won't last long. We already have to move our cars during most high tides and a lot of us have converted our first floors to garages and moved our utilities to the second floor.

We know that in twenty to thirty years, sea level rise will make our homes uninhabitable."

"What will you do then?"

"I'm so damn old it won't affect me. But most of my neighbors will have to think about moving to higher ground. We are tough old buzzards out here, nobody wants to move, but storm by storm Mother Nature will solve the problem in her own way and on her own terms."

"Thanks, I think I have my lede."

CHAPTER 23

Editorial Meeting

Boston, Massachusetts
July 9, 2022

"The Supreme Court has appointed itself as the decision maker on climate policy… I cannot think of many things more frightening!"

Justice Elena Kagen, Supreme Court
Dissenting Opinion
West Virginia vs. EPA
July 2022

Finbar Muldoon switched on Zoom on his laptop.

Finbar: "Hi gang, thanks for attending."

Ericka: "As if we have a choice!"

Finbar: "I'll ignore that Ericka. Now what I'd like to do is pick all your brains about how we should cover the Supreme Court's EPA decision.

I find it particularly ironic that the decision was made 50 years after the publication of MIT's Limits to Growth book and 25 years after the Massachusetts case that determined that the EPA could regulate carbon dioxide as a pollutant. Either one of those anniversary stories would give us a local angle."

Gregor: "But wasn't Limits to Growth debunked?"

Ericka: "Totally! By the oil companies and their intellectual enablers, by the Catholic Church because of its stand on population, and by economists because they think of growth as the bedrock of capitalism.

But mostly it pissed off all these groups because they saw scientists encroaching on their turf."

Sylvia: "Most of my red diaper relatives thought the whole thing was a scam perpetrated by capitalist elites to trick workers into believing that a proletariat paradise was only a pipe dream."

Finbar: "OK, OK. Ericka?"

Ericka: "The bottom line is that the eggheads had it right. Their model predicted that if we continue guzzling oil and having too many babies, the economy and society will collapse in thirty years."

Gregor: "That model was so old they were still using computer punch cards for God's sake!"

Sylvia: "You know what they say about models, none of them are accurate, but some of them are useful."

Ericka: "The model would have been useful if anyone had heeded its warnings. Instead they just fiddled and diddled for half a century."

Sylvia: "The Supreme Court decision will set us back another decade and we need that decade to make the transition to carbon-free energy."

Ericka: "The people who are making the day-to-day decisions about things like sea level rise say that trying to prepare for the crisis is more important than trying to avoid it. They have to make real world decisions about which towns and cities are worth saving and which to sacrifice to the rising seas."

Finbar: "What if we concentrate on a single city like Phoenix that is quickly becoming uninhabitable? It has already had over 20 days with over 110-degree temperatures so far this year."

Ericka: "You are always going on about how some city or country is going to become uninhabitable. Nonsense. Humans are nothing if not adaptable. People will just start living underground and using more air conditioners or raise their beach houses up on stilts."

Sylvia: "The problem is humans are too adaptable. If we weren't, the human population would be a lot smaller and clustered in a small band of temperate locations."

Ericka: "The environmental crisis is nothing if not a crisis about how we live, and I think some people are starting to get that. They want to make things better. They are composting, having fewer babies, eating lower in the food pyramid, and buying electric cars."

Sylvia: "You can't just switch fuels and change light bulbs. You have to change our political system as well. I think we should write about the next election."

Finbar: "Let's let the political writers deal with that!"

Sylvia: "There you go erecting those silos again. It's the gestalt you have to change."

Gregor: "There you go with your big fancy words Sylvia. What the hell is a gestalt?"

Ericka: "Think of it as the whole ball of wax, Gregor."

Sylvia: "The bottom line is that the Supreme Court has set itself up as the final arbiter on climate change and they don't know bubkis about it. I think we should start with Justice Kagan's comment that she can't think of anything more frightening than having the Supreme Court have the last word about climate change."

Finbar: "And I'm afraid that has to be the last word for this meeting. Thanks for your input. Talk to you next week."

"God willing and the creek don't rise," sighed Ericka before signing off.

CHAPTER 24

Forest Rendezvous

50 miles from Nova Kakhovka, Ukraine
July 12, 2022

Mist hung in the trees as Petra eased her mother's Skoda to the side of a heavily forested road southeast of Kyiv.

"What are we doing here?" asked Gregor.

"I want you to meet a friend."

"Who's that?"

"You'll see."

Two minutes later a boxy looking rocket launcher lurched out of the fog. Walking behind it was a familiar face.

"Who's your friend, Petra?"

"Zelya, I'd like you to meet Gregor McFadden. He writes for the Boston Globe."

"I've read your stuff. You're doing a good job telling our story. Thank you!"

"Bozhe med, it is an honor to meet you, Mr. President. Petra never told me who she was getting her inside information from!"

"She's good at keeping secrets."

"I'll say."

Petra smiled.

"But here, I'd like you to meet the commander of one of the High Mobility Artillery Rocket Systems you gave us. See, it was made in Dallas by Lockheed. Last night these guys used it to destroy an ammunition warehouse in the Russian occupied city of Nova Kakhovka.

Thanks to your country we have these launchers. They have made all the difference to us. Now we have a chance against the Russian bastards ... if I may say so."

"Of course you can."

"You see they don't know how to use pallets and cranes to move their equipment. They load and unload everything by hand, so they are sitting ducks for our rockets. We make a point of moving everyday so they can't get a bead on our positions."

"I saw the satellite images of that strike. It was a pinpoint hit."

"Yes, all it left was one small crater. Our old rockets would have spread out all over the map."

"How far is Nova Kakhovka from here?"

"Let's just say it is 50 miles and leave it at that."

"Fair enough."

"Other units made similar hits in Luhansk and Donetsk as well as Melitopol and Zaporizhzhia last week. It is starting to slow the Russians down."

"Our harpoon missiles have also destroyed a Russian tugboat supplying Snake Island, so we have been able to push the invaders off the island. Soon we will be able to remove some of the mines so that we can start exporting our grain to Africa and the Middle East again. That will give them badly needed food and give us badly needed money, so we can continue to buy more ammunition to fight this war."

That night Petra slept in Gregor's bed in Kyiv.

 "I love the sound of rain on the roof."

"Yes, so much better than the sound of incoming rounds.

I want to thank you for an incredible interview and another incredible day. How did you set it up?"

"I have my ways."

"You do! Anyway, it is good to be back in Kyiv."

"Yes, this is where I belong."

"I hope where we both belong."

"Yes, where we both belong."

CHAPTER 25

Space Balls and Mockingbirds

Ipswich, Massachusetts
July 17, 2022

Ericka lounged on Leyla's bed savoring the early morning calls of birds while wondering how she was ever going to write about the heat waves in the U.S., Europe and Asia ... to say nothing of the Covid pandemic that Dr. Fauci had just admitted was going to be with us for the rest of our lives.

Ericka had met Leyla when she was walking around Great Neck, the hill of glacial debris rising above Ipswich Marsh. She had been admiring some daffodils when Leyla emerged from weeding; hot, sweaty, laughing and incredibly gorgeous.

Leyla had dropped off a vase of fresh daffodils on Ericka's back steps the next day, and Ericka had reciprocated with several home-grown geraniums, which seemed a little like bringing coals to Newcastle.

Leyla's house overlooked the marsh and acres of vine-covered forest. Soon, they were spending every night sitting on Leyla's deck sipping red wine and nibbling smoked mussels, while prehistoric looking herons and flocks of snowy egrets swirled and tumbled down through the thick trees to their roost beside a glistening green fresh water pond.

But their favorite creature was what they called their mockingbird with an attitude. He sat on the top of a telephone pole in front of Leyla's house and regaled them with his rich repertoire of bird-calls: first a cardinal, then a robin, a blue jay, then a northern flicker.

Occasionally he would throw in the calls of feeding terns and a willet before mimicking the FedEx man's backup alarm ... just for effect. It seemed that if he felt they were not paying close enough attention, the mockingbird would fly four feet into the air, land and call even louder.

Ericka opened the morning news. Matthew Cappucci had the lead story in the Washington Post. The Harvard trained meteorologist had been writing for the Post since he was 18 years old. The older generation of weather forecasters had cast a skeptical eye on global warming but as they died off they had been replaced by the new Young Turk wunderkinds who wrote knowledgably about climate change.

"Yup, science writing is advancing funeral by funeral," muttered Ericka to herself.

"What was that?"

"Matthew has a series of maps that shows the heat waves advancing across the United States, Europe and Asia. Hundreds of people have already died in Spain and Portugal where 115-degree temperatures have fueled wildfires along the entire Mediterranean coast. England is expected to set an all-time record tomorrow."

"It is all just so frightening."

"Meanwhile temperatures have already hit 113 degrees in Texas and Oklahoma. A third heat wave will heat up India, Tibet and Pakistan until it causes a thermal low to draw in moist air from the Bay of Bengal, which will bring on the monsoons. But it is all happening so much faster than the experts anticipated."

"What are you going to do about it?"

"Well, I've written about nuclear fusion and carbon capture and those could be game changers, but they will take too long to achieve anything. But now I have to get ready to cover one of MIT's fringier ideas."

Ericka reluctantly left Leyla and the mockingbird to drive into Cambridge for her appointment with Professor Carlo Ratti, leaving herself an extra half hour to figure out MIT's confusing method of numbering its many buildings and offices. She figured it was designed that way to thwart errant journalists.

At last, she found the Senseable Cities Center housed in MIT's

Media Lab. Dr. Ratti showed her the lab's proposal to inflate a number of film-like silicon space bubbles that would be joined together in a matrix the size of Brazil.

"The concept was first proposed by the astronomer Roger Angel."

"Roger Angel, an astronomer? You've got to be kidding me."

"Actually, he was quite well known. He suggested using a flotilla of small space vehicles to block the sun's rays from reaching the earth. We have altered his concept to include a raft of silicon bubbles that we would send to the L1 LaGrange point. That is where the earth's and the sun's gravitational fields cancel each other so the bubbles will just float stationary in space."

"What if they don't?"

"In the event some of the space bubbles do fall out of their LaGrange orbit, we will also deploy a small spacecraft to keep them in line."

That evening Ericka climbed the spiral staircase back up to Leyla's deck to take pictures of the egrets coming in to roost. But every once in a while, an osprey would fly by at eye level holding a menhaden or wriggling flounder.

One osprey flew just over the head of the mockingbird and gave its intimidating high warning whistle which was instantly mimicked by the cheeky little mockingbird to the delight of his human audience.

CHAPTER 26

The January 6th Hearings

Ipswich, Massachusetts
July 21, 2022

Ericka switched on the January 6th Congressional committee hearings while Sylvia served up a platter of palm hearts, home grown lettuce, smoked Gouda and bluefish pate.

"I tell my kids it's my special 'summer salad,' but it really just leftovers from the night before."

Matthew Pottinger appeared on the screen. Trump's former national security advisor for China was explaining what he had been doing on the night of the riots.

"I disagree with almost all of his politics but I still find him pretty impressive," said Ericka.

"Yes, he was my ace in the hole when I was writing about the Covid origins."

"How was that?'

"Well, he grew up around here and studied Mandarin at UMass so he was fluent when he was writing for Reuters. It allowed him to get to know all the Chinese doctors and researchers dealing with the SARS epidemic.

But his work also convinced him that China believed that democracies like the United States were in decline and that their system of autocratic capitalism would eventually replace Western democracies. He felt so intensely that democracy was worth fighting for, that he signed up for the Marine Corps and served in Kabul."

"Unlike so many of these other weasely politicians he actually lived by his convictions. Didn't he also meet his wife in Kabul?"

"Yup, Yen Duong is a virologist who escaped Vietnam by boat."

"She must have helped him when Covid struck."

"He was perfectly positioned to know what was going on. He could read tweets from Chinese friends saying that an accident had occurred in one of the Wuhan labs, and that some people were testing positive for a new coronavirus disease but some were presenting without symptoms. So his friends warned Pottinger that the new virus could enter the United States without even being detected."

"And he told that to the President?"

"In no uncertain terms!"

"Pottinger also told me that one kindly old Chinese doctor told him that Covid was a respiratory disease and that he should drink hot tea to kill the viruses before they were swept down into his lungs."

"Makes some sense actually."

"Yeah, anyway he scalded his throat from drinking tea every time he was exposed. And of course, the White House was a super spreader site where Trump humiliated him for wearing a mask."

"So how did your Covid book finally work out?"

"Horrible. It was actually the first book to investigate the idea that Covid could have come out because of a lab accident."

"That should have helped."

"But it came out when Trump was still in office so the media wouldn't touch it, and nobody read it. It reminded me of what my relatives went through during the McCarthy era."

"Really!"

"It was a shameful handling of what should have always been a sober scientific debate. But it showed me that scientists and the media can be as tribal as anyone else."

"What do you think about the lab leak idea now?"

"I never thought of it as a conspiracy theory, just a scientific theory to be proven or not proven, that's simply how science works. Unfortunately, facts were lost in the maelstrom of political paranoia surrounding Trump.

If he hadn't used China as a political foil I think the Chinese researchers and the U.S. agencies that funded them would have been more forthcoming and admitted that someone had made a simple mistake. Happens all the time when you are doing cutting edge research.

That's doubly true for medical science. Years ago the dean of Harvard Medical School congratulated the graduating class for all their hard work but cautioned them, 'Half of what you have just learned will be proved wrong in the next few years, but unfortunately we can't tell you which half.'"

"So, you think the same is true for Covid's origins? The jury is still out?"

"Yes, you would think that if it emerged from nature, researchers would have discovered the host organism or a definitive gene sequence by now.

But they haven't. They have proposed a complicated series of up to two dozen instances when the coronavirus spilled over from animals in the Wuhan market to humans. But they haven't identified any of the animals that actually harbored the virus.

Plus, you have this hugely improbable coincidence that the virus just happened to appear outside the very lab where researchers were studying the virus, and the bats that harbor them. But the bats only occur in nature a thousand miles away.

I still find it just as plausible if not more probable that one of the researchers studying the virus accidentally contracted the virus and infected people in the market and the Union Hospital where he would have been treated.

At least the NIH is investigating just how risky that sort of research is. If they stop funding risky Gain of Function research, we will all be much safer."

"Didn't Pottinger convince Trump to ban flights from China?"

"Yes, it was considered xenophobic at the time, but the ban would have slowed things down if it had been done right away. I salute Pottinger for trying to work within the system."

"Didn't you do the same sort of thing when you wrote your

book about the horseshoe crab industry, and how their blood is used to make sure vaccines are free from bacterial contamination?"

"Funny you should say that. The other day I was in Woods Hole and happened to bump into someone who used to work in the Crab Lab. He told me that when he worked there nobody was allowed to mention my name. But after he resigned, he realized I had had it right all along.

He even told me about an incident where the cooling system in one of their trucks delivering horseshoe crabs from Virginia had broken down. When they lifted up the back door they were assailed with the smell of thousands of dead and dying horseshoe crabs. Of course, the incident was never reported and the figures were never added to their official mortality figures."

"Suboptimal outcome!"

"To be sure. Their people weren't just making mistakes, they were knowingly hiding the fact that they were killing far more crabs than they were reporting."

"So, they were killing the goose that lays the golden egg!"

"Precisely."

"Didn't one of our rival papers run an article about a South Carolina company getting permission to collect horseshoe crabs up here?"

"It was a good article, but unfortunately it missed the point. A lot of people got their names in the paper, but nobody is looking at the real issue. The reason the South Carolina company is coming up here is that they were collecting horseshoe crabs when they were laying their eggs, so they were not being replaced by the next generation of crabs.

The same thing happened up here when the crabs were being collected when they were spawning in the Cape Cod National Seashore."

"Wasn't that practice stopped after the collectors lost a federal court case?"

"Yup, but now there is so much pressure on using horseshoe

crab blood to test the Covid vaccines, that they are collecting spawning crabs again."

"You're lucky you've lived long enough to see your book vindicated. I'm not sure we will ever know how Covid came about. Even though nobody read the book, it whetted my appetite to write about bigger issues."

"Not a bad thing."

"Yup it's like a friend of mine down in Woods Hole who used to say he always fished with a huge lure because if he wasn't going to catch a fish, he would rather not catch a big fish than a small fish… That's also why he won a Noble Prize!"

"Albert Zent-Georgyi, right?"

"Yes, we have to be like him and Pottinger, just do our best to explain science and the scientific method. But we also have to remember that science is just like any other beat. If you discover that something doesn't smell right, your job is to track it down. And the most important thing is to pursue your story is with courage, integrity and the facts."

"For sure."

CHAPTER 27

Joe Manchin Fools Mitch McConnell

Washington D.C.
July 28, 2022

"Americans always do the right thing after they have exhausted
every other possibility."
Erroneously attributed to
Winston Churchill

Finbar was delighted to see that Senators Joe Manchin and Mitch
McConnell had reached a compromise on what they called their
Inflation Reduction Act. If passed, the bill promised to unlock trillions of dollars of investments in renewable energy. It would
change the world as other countries followed suit, so they would
not miss out on the new industries. He couldn't wait to email his
most cynical reporter.

"Aren't you thrilled about today's announcement Ericka?"

"Not really. It just ensures the continuation of our car culture."

"It promises to reduce carbon emissions 40% by 2030."

"But it will just lock in our inefficient car culture for decades."

"How so?"

"It is all about subsidizing electric cars and batteries."

"Isn't that good?"

"Not really. Driving an EV down the highway uses as much
electricity as air conditioning 5 or 6 homes. What we really need is
for people to walk more, drive less, and use things like electric bicy-
cles and small cars around the neighborhood."

"You are such a downer, Ericka. That's just not politically
feasible in today's world. But how did the bill come about?"

"With a whole lot of theater. Mitch McConnell was going on and on that if the Democrats didn't stop telling the Republicans that they would not pass the semiconductor bill, the Republicans would refuse to pass any climate legislation."

"How did the Democrats react?"

"Senator Manchin flipped out or at least pretended to flip out, saying McConnell was just as bad as the Lefties who were threatening to hold up the infrastructure bill."

"What happened?"

"Days later he walked out of Schumer's climate bill meeting. I and most other reporters were convinced the climate bill was dead and apparently McConnell did as well. The Senate passed the semiconductor bill and four hours later Manchin and Schumer announced they had a deal."

"McConnell must have been fuming!"

"Yup, he's not used to Democrats beating him at his own game."

"Wasn't Manchin in some kind of hot water for appropriating money to establish a wildlife refuge near his West Virginia condo?"

"That was a nothing burger cooked up by some of my environmental colleagues. Manchin is an old-fashioned hunter-fisher environmentalist. If he can get funding for a refuge that will benefit wildlife and everyone who visits it, who cares that it is near his condo?"

"Wasn't Kennedy criticized for funding the Cape Cod National Seashore near his family compound in Hyannis?"

"Yes, and it was the best thing that ever happened to the Cape and the millions of people who use the National Seashore every year. By now the Cape would be covered with coastal developments if it hadn't been for the establishment of the Seashore."

"So you do like the Inflation Reduction Act."

"The bill is not great but at least it will give humanity a fighting chance."

"From you, I'd call that high praise indeed. Think you can get an interview with Manchin?"

"I'm pretty high on his fecal roster right now."
"We need something for Tuesday's edition."
"You're pushing it Muldoon, you're pushing it."

CHAPTER 28

"The Good Guys Are Starting to Win Again."

Odessa, Ukraine
August 1, 2022

"While Russia takes the lives of others … we allow them to survive."
Volodymr Zelensky
July 31, 2022

"It sends chills down my spine," said Petra as she and Gregor stood on the dock watching tugboats ease the grain ship *Razoni* out of Odessa Harbor.

"Those are the pilot boats that will guide her down through the mine free corridor to Istanbul and on to Lebanon."

"It wouldn't have happened if your country hadn't sent us rocket systems to recapture Snake Island and knock out the Russian tugboats. Last night a drone landed on the headquarters of their Black Sea fleet. The Russians responded by killing Oleksiy Vadutursky. He started Nibulon, a Ukranian company that exports food to Africa and the Middle East."

"Bloody Putin using food as a weapon, for God's sake."

"But if the *Razoni* gets through it will be a huge success. And hopefully it will be followed by the 15 other blockaded ships. Selling their grain will give us the money we need to rebuild Ukraine."

"I understand Ukranian troops are also poised to recapture Kherson."

" Yes, last Tuesday they used another HIMARS multiple rocket launcher to knock out the Actonivskiy Bridge, leaving the Russians sitting like ducks in Kharkiv."

"It's very risky but it will be a huge morale booster if it works."

"Yes Kharkiv was the first and largest city the Russians captured, but now they have outrun their supply lines.

They are getting so scared they are firing their artillery pieces from the Zaporizhzhia nuclear power plant so we can't fire back."

"Cowards!"

"It would also be a morale booster for some of your more wobbly allies that are starting to question their decisions to cut back on Russian gas this winter. But I want to show you another hopeful story."

"Good, I need a hopeful story. I'm getting sick of all these unhopeful ones."

Just down the road, Petra pulled into the Odessa Aquarium.

"What's here?"

"Your other morale booster story."

"All I see is four dolphins swimming around a pool."

"That one is 'Dream'. She was born during the bombardment of Kharkiv."

"It must have scared her to death."

"Almost, dolphins can actually feel the pressure of the incoming missiles before they explode, so they were all terrified. Most of the pod was evacuated last April, but Dream was too young so they kept her and her family in Kharkiv."

"How did they get them here?"

"Their trainer, a veterinarian, and a driver drove them in a truck for over ten hours. They had to keep spraying them with water so they wouldn't overheat.

Or panic like Horace the elephant in Kyiv Zoo. His trainer moved his family into the zoo so he could stay up all night giving Horace melons and sedatives to keep him calm during the bombing."

"Frightful what we do to such gentle innocent animals."

"But now Dream and her family is in Odessa and our grain is sailing off to Africa to feed the world."

"And our American Senate may pass the most extensive environmental legislation the world has ever seen."

"It feels like the world is coming to its senses and the good guys are finally winning again."

"We will see. We will see."

CHAPTER 29

The Future is in Our Hands

Ipswich, Massachusetts
August 10, 2022

"Up ahead they's a thousan' lives we might live, she said, but when it comes, it'll on'y be one."

"Grapes of Wrath"
John Steinbeck
1939

Ericka awoke breathless and exhausted with a throbbing headache. It had been a double Ambien night and promised to be a double Tylenol day. The problem was the weather. It had never cooled down from last night's 90-degree temperatures and they were facing several more days of the same. It felt like she couldn't catch her next breath even as she got out of bed.

Outside, the giant orange sun heaved itself out of the ocean and beat down hard on the dust and bristly brown fields on either side of Great Neck. She grabbed her walking stick and trudged slowly uphill.

It was 5 in the morning, so she figured she still had time to climb up to Leyla's house before the heat became too oppressive.

Last year Ericka had to be rushed to the ER and be shocked back into sinus rhythm after collapsing on this same hill from dehydration and atrial fibrillation.

The town had passed a mandatory watering ban because of the ongoing drought, but if she hurried, she should be able to empty Leyla's rain barrels to water the garden before the ozone polluted air became too deadly.

When she finished watering, she snapped a photo of the rising sun and posted it on Facebook. A denier posted,

"Just another hot, dry summer."

She knew she shouldn't, but she shot back, "Yup just like the droughts, floods, fires and heat waves that have left over 100 million Americans under heat advisories. That would all be impossible without global warming.

All this has happened after only a single degree of global warming and it is a fraction of what will occur if emissions are left unchecked."

"That's just egghead talk."

"Could be, but true all the same."

"Manchin's so-called inflation fighting bill is going to ruin our economy."

"Actually, it should help supply thousands of new jobs and trillions of dollars in investments."

"Even if it works, we are going to continue to have ever increasing extreme events throughout our lifetime and into those of our children and grandchildren."

"But if we don't take these steps the future will be truly frightening, chimed in another commentator, "and a three degree increase in global temperature won't be three times worse, it will be exponentially worse, and the number of heat deaths will be that much higher."

"So is there any reason for hope?"

"I just hope we realize that the inflation fighting bill is far cheaper than trying to adapt to an ever more feverish planet."

She knew she was getting on her high horse, but Ericka couldn't stop herself.

"Each of us has the ability to rewrite the future. It is precisely at this late hour when the darkness is most intense that we can stand up against this madness and sprint toward the light."

Her comment elicited several eye rolls, but she pressed on. "As Ma said in The Grapes of Wrath, 'Up ahead they's a thousand lives we might live, but when it comes it'll only be one.'"

"That book should be banned, but it proves my point we have always had droughts and floods."

"That's right, global warming started kicking in about the Thirties, but we didn't have the instruments to measure carbon dioxide then so we figured it was just a fluke. Now, however, summer droughts spreading across our country like a big dark stain every summer."

Ericka couldn't wait for Leyla to return from attending to her ninety-eight year old mother sweltering dangerously in New York City. With the heat wave, they would have a lot to talk about.

CHAPTER 30

The Bill

Cape Cod, Massachusetts
August 16, 2022

"You'd never want to wake up and find yourself in Cook County Hospital. The building looks as huge, grey and battered as a vanquished and abandoned old battleship run aground on the shattered streets just west of Chicago's Loop. The hallways and waiting rooms-- there's no nicer way to put this -- are thick with sick people who have also run aground and seem abandoned to waiting, limping, straining, coughing, sighing, and sweating, bleeding and crying."

Scott Simon, Weekend Edition,
National Public Radio, 1994

Ericka invited Sylvia and Leyla to her house on Cape Cod to watch President Biden sign the historic climate bill, but he was taking his time.

"You know I've been waiting my whole career for this day."

"How did it start?" asked Leyla.

"I always loved nature and writing. I'm afflicted with both the writing bug and biophilia."

"Sounds kinda kinky."

"I actually think the two are genetically linked."

"But when did you become aware of our modern understanding of the environment?"

"Many years ago. I was sitting beside Al Gore while a visiting professor showed a bunch of us undergraduates a graph with a jagged line of carbon dioxide rising ominously to the right. He explained that it would inexorably lead to the greenhouse effect, global warming, heat waves and sea level rise.

At the time we figured that since scientists knew about the problem that politicians would have it all solved it by the time we graduated.

And what happened? Zilch, nada, nothing until today."

"What was that course?"

"It was a special seminar. I'm still ticked at Harvard for accepting Gore for credit while I had to take it pass fail."

"And look what happened to Gore."

"Yeah, he lost a presidential election."

"But won a Nobel Prize and an Oscar."

"Yeah, yeah don't rub it in."

"That seminar had other repercussions. Because of his affiliation with Harvard, New York Senator Pat Moynihan knew about the seminar and wrote a memo to President Nixon explaining how increased atmospheric carbon dioxide would lead to sea level rise writing, 'Goodbye New York. And Goodbye Washington D.C. for that matter.'"

"Had a way with words, didn't he?"

"Indeed, and Nixon passed the Clean Air and Clean Water Acts but he never did anything about Moynihan's little carbon dioxide problem."

Neither did Ford, Carter, Reagan, Clinton, Obama, Trump or both Bushes."

"Why not?"

"They all tried to solve the problem with taxes on things like oil, gasoline and coal use, but people never vote to tax themselves, or elect representatives to do the same."

"So how did it happen?"

"Biden; bless his heart, switched from using sticks to carrots. He stuck to his campaign mantra, 'When I think of green energy I think of good jobs.'

And it was Joe Manchin, of all people, who broke the logjam by selling the bill as an inflation fighting measure."

"That's a stretch."

"It was, but it worked."

Leyla looked around, "What about you Sylvia? How did you get into medicine?"

"The only occupations open to girls in those days was teaching or being a nurse, but I had the audacity to think I could be a doctor.

Went to the University of Chicago and trained at Cook County Hospital. It was the largest and oldest public hospital in the world. It was a big grey dysfunctional beast that perfectly fit my mix of idealism and impatience. We saw everything from gunshot wounds to tropical diseases and our patients taught us about their lives and how racist and unfair medicine was … and still is.

Most of our patients were dumped on us from private hospitals because most of the poor Black patients didn't have health insurance. Mothers and children died because the private hospitals turned them away."

"It must have been awful."

"Awful and fulfilling at the same time. But it was also one of the best ways to get burned out.

The final straw came when the hospital shifted to electronic medical records. At the end of a grueling day we still had to spend two more hours doing our frigging notes. I figured I could do more good writing about medicine than being a doctor in the trenches."

"It makes me feel guilty that I have always worked in beautiful spots, like here," said Ericka.

"But this is where the pedal meets the metal, where people are directly affected by environmental problems. It used to be that you were isolated from environmental problems in cities and could ignore them.

No more. Now our cities are hot, polluted and threatened with sea level rise, and again it is the minority-owned areas that are the dumping grounds for our worst environmental problems."

"But Sylvia, don't you ever miss medicine?"

"I miss the intellectual challenges and working with patients, but the other day my one of my kids told me she was thinking of applying to medical school.

I told her OMDB, over my dead body! 'It's a deal!' she replied."

"Now she would make a great writer," said Leyla.

Sylvia pointed toward the screen. "Look there he goes. He's signing the bill. No turning back now. It sends shivers down my spine."

"Frankly I still have some doubts about whether his build back bigger and better approach will work. I've always believed you have make sacrifices and cut back to preserve the environment, but it seems build back bigger and better is the only thing that the public can agree on, so I'm willing to give it a chance," said Ericka.

"Until 2030 when emissions are supposed to be down by 40%. That's only 8 short years away," replied Sylvia.

"Yup, a lot of people will get short-term jobs, a few people will get filthy rich, and it could lead to another gilded era as entirely new industries come online," added Ericka.

"What about carbon removal?" asked Leyla.

"A pipe dream. It won't stop the global warming that is already baked into the system because of the huge volume of carbon dioxide that is already in the air," Ericka responded.

"Then do you think we will realize that carrots aren't enough?"

"Perhaps. But I just hope it won't be too late."

"And I just hope I'll still be around to see what happens. What a mess we are leaving for our children and grandchildren."

"And great grandchildren," added Ericka.

CHAPTER 31

Svarog

Zaporizhia, Ukraine
August 21, 2022

"The war in Ukraine began with Crimea and must end with Crimea…"

Volodymyr Zelensky
August 17, 2022

On August 18th Gregor and Petra interviewed President Zelensky's aide, Mykhailo Podolynk who insisted that Ukraine had nothing to do with some mysterious blasts at Crimea's Saki airfield.

"Of course not, what would we have to do with such explosions?" said Podolynk trying to suppress a smile.

The explosions had sent so many Russian tourists scurrying out of their seaside cabanas to escape back across the clogged Kerch Straits Bridge that Russia had to shut the bridge down.

Putin had made it abundantly clear that he considered Crimea sacred ground and Judgment Day would descend on anyone who had the temerity to attack it.

But Gregor and Petra were about to meet someone who had such temerity. He met them disguised behind dark glasses and a death mask gaiter at a Georgian restaurant in Zaporizhia.

"You may call me Partisan Svarog."

"How do you come by such a name?"

"Svarog was the Slavic god of fire and investigator of monogamous relationships. In real life I teach."

"Tell me what you are doing in Crimea."

"Oh, we sneak down darkened alleys, set off explosives, identify targets for our drones and rockets. We have even been known to blow up rail lines and assassinate officials who we think are collaborators."

"Podolynk says partisans had nothing to do with attacking the Saki airfield."

"Of course we had a hand in that, plus the strike that destroyed 8 jets and caused the Russians to move 38 of their aircraft to airbases farther away from the front lines."

"Did your colleagues assassinate the daughter of Putin's right hand man in Moscow?"

"Assassinating Darya Durgina would be a big mistake. I think it was an inside job done by someone fed up with Putin's war."

"So what is your ultimate goal?"

"We want to scare the occupiers, to show them that they are not at home, that they should not settle in and not sleep comfortably."

"Has it worked?"

"We just caused the Russians to fire the head of their Black Sea Command. That should put them off balance for weeks if not months."

"What do you plan to do in the future?"

Svarog rolled his eyes in disbelief.

"Ok, Ok, I know you can't tell me, but what would you like to do?"

"We really want to knock out the Kerch Straits Bridge.

The Russians built the bridge to bolster their claims that they had captured Crimea and that it was a part of greater Russia. It's 12 miles long, the longest in Europe and the longest bridge ever built by Russia.

Every day thousands of Russian tourists cross it to hike in the Crimean Mountains and swim in the Black Sea. But Russia also sends trains across the bridge with ammunition to attack our troops."

"So, knocking it out would be a huge win for you and yet another red-faced humiliation for Russia."

"Exactly! It has huge historical significance. The Straits were originally part of the Silk Road and the Nazis built a cargo ropeway across them and started to build a bridge but blew it up before they retreated. We would like to hand Russia such a soul-destroying defeat ourselves."

"Can I join you on your next sabotage mission?"

"I fear it would be a suicide mission for you my friend. We appreciate what you are doing and want you to stay alive so you can continue to tell our story to the world."

CHAPTER 32

Will Dinosaurs Inherit
our Warming Planet?

Cambridge, Massachusetts
August 23, 2022

Ericka entered Harvard's Museum of Natural History through its basement side door and was immediately assailed with the smell of formaldehyde that was so intimately linked with memories of the intellectual awakenings she had experienced in this same building decades before.

Inside the foyer she was surrounded by huge plaster casts of dinosaur tracks while the stern visage of Louis Agassiz stared down upon her. Did he finally deem her qualified to pass on scientific knowledge to future generations? She doubted it as she had as a young undergraduate decades before.

She made her way between a languishing hippopotamus and two new lion cubs preserved forever in their glass cases, then mounted the cast iron staircase near a gorilla beating his chest and passed under a suspended skeleton of a sperm whale, to ring the bell of the dinosaur department.

No one took particular notice of her entrance. They were locked in one of their infamous discussions, loud witty, boisterous, and opinionated. Their arguments swung from digging fossils in China to the impact of the new climate bill.

Fred Pierce was in the lead; "The reigning scenario is that this so-called inflation fighting bill will start to remove enough carbon dioxide emissions so our own adaptable species can survive."

"Rubbish!" exclaimed a colleague.

"Not without a huge population crash to wipe the slate clean," said another.

"What about Elon Musk's idea of sending a few select human beings to colonize another planet?" asked Ericka tentatively.

"Species exceptionalism at best. Immoral at worst!"

"Why use all our hospitable planet's resources to colonize an inhospitable planet. Why not clean up our own planet first?"

"Of course, in the greater scheme of things, our ecosystem is far more important than our destructive little species. As far as we know, it is the only ecosystem that harbors life. The universe and our planet would be much better off if the dominate organisms were fish, birds, dinosaurs or helpful bacteria, certainly not humans like Elon Musk!"

Dr. Pierce forged ahead, "We are paleontologists for God's sake. Let's project as far into the future as possible, while we look back at the past. The public thinks that only animals like cockroaches and horseshoe crabs will survive. But I think we could see the return of large dinosaurs. That's what you see if you look at the fossil record."

"We certainly have lots of dinosaurs to start with, " said her doctoral student Joan Samos.

"What do you mean," asked Ericka?

"When you walk out your door what do you see? Birds. They are just small flying dinosaurs biding their time for the climate to warm so they can grow larger again. There are 400 billion of them and only 8 billion of us. We are still in the Age of the Dinosaurs."

"And birds are already preadapted to live in a changing world. They can fly, and most of them already migrate so they can move to cooler habitats as the world heats up. We have already seen lots of birds expand north like the cardinals and turkey vultures that you never used to see in New England before the 1960's."

"Darwin showed that birds could rapidly evolve different features like stout bills to feed on seeds, and thin bills to feed on insects."

"Birds are also small which helps them retain heat in cold environments, but they could become much larger as the world warms."

"Yes, they did this once before. Millions of years ago there were lots of synaptid mammals and relatively few small lizards. But as the world warmed, reptiles slowly evolved into dinosaurs that grew larger and larger until they were wiped out during the asteroid extinction 60 million years ago.

Paleontologists used to think this was because the extinction of most of the synaptids allowed the reptiles to take over new habitats. But we found that it was the rise in temperatures that led to the explosion of reptiles that led the world into the Dinosaur Age."

"Of course, evolution is a crap shoot. If you knocked on the Mammal Department door they would tell you that marine mammals will dominate the warming world because they are smart, live in a cooler environment, and can migrate to even cooler waters.

They would say that all dolphins would have to do is evolve hands so they could manipulate their environment."

"So, they could screw up the oceans and evolve back into the terrestrial creatures they once were."

"And if you knocked on the Malacology Department door the clam guys would insist that some kind of squid or octopus would take over the warmer world."

"And the fish people would tell you about their epaulette sharks that have evolved paddlelike legs in response to global warming. The legs allow them to hobble from one tidepool to another as the pools run out of oxygen as the seasons get warmer."

"But isn't this all idle speculation?"

"Not if you are a paleontologist. We get paid to find out what happened millions of years ago. You writers can speculate what it might all mean for the future. But for God's sake don't quote us on any of this!"

CHAPTER 33

Forever Chemicals

Ipswich MA
August 25, 2022

"If you visit American city,
You will find it very pretty.
Just two things of which you must beware
Don't drink the water and don't breathe the air!"

Tom Lehrer
"Pollution"
January 1, 1965

Ericka called Sylvia, "Did you see that The Journal of Environmental Science and Technology just released a study that warned that rainwater is now unsafe to drink anywhere in the world, because of forever chemicals?"

"Incredible, isn't it?"

"Yes, I remember several years ago I was listening to a boring lecture about forever chemicals in the Merrimack River. I wasn't paying very much attention until the lecturer happened to mention that the military was banning the use of fire-fighting foam because it causes cancer.

Whoa, all of a sudden, she had my full attention. I explained that my town has a local tradition where the fire department sprays all the town's kids and asked it could possibly be the same foam. It was."

"Did you write about it?"

"No. I didn't want to be the local crank who rained on one of her town's beloved traditions."

"So, you didn't?"

"Didn't have to. Covid came along so they cancelled the tradition. Last fall I was on the beach and happened to run into our new young fire chief and told him about the lecture. He assured me the town would never again foam kids on his watch."

"But you missed out on an important article."

"Sometimes it's better to solve things quietly."

"Not very journalistic of you."

"No, but I like to be able to live in peace in my own town."

"It's much easier to whack the President in Washington than a local selectman you might see in the market the next day."

"What are you going to do now that it is a worldwide problem?"

"Why write it up of course! Now that we have some distance on the problem."

"Yeah, like planetary distance."

"How come scientists just found out about this?"

"They didn't, but it turns out that the researchers who have been studying forever chemicals found them to be a lot more toxic than they originally thought, so they have lowered the standards for the safe amounts of the chemicals. Now the new standards are below the amount of the chemicals found in rainwater, the ocean and soils."

"What are the chemicals exactly?"

"Per and polyfluoroalkyl substances, PFAS for short."

"Sorry I asked."

"Some guy put the F in Fluorine and the C in Carbon to come up with "Forever Chemicals" which is a lot easier to remember and emphasizes their persistence in the environment."

"Where do they come from?"

"Originally 3M and DuPont made them from petroleum. But now several spinoff companies manufacture them. Those companies were basically created so DuPont could declare bankruptcy and not be sued."

"Typical. Where do we pick these PFAS up?"

"Everywhere. A local teacher had one of her undergraduates do a day in the life of a typical college student. The student tested things around her campus for PFAS. She found them in her shoes, on her rug, in her furniture, cosmetics, lotions and eye drops, as well as in her clothes, in her non-stick frying pan and in the wrappers of her fast food hamburgers. And of course it is also in her drinking water and blood. 99% of people all over the world have them in their blood."

"So, everyone should be worried?"

"Some more than others. If you live near one of the 200 military bases where they trained with fire-fighting foams you should be very concerned about cancers."

"Like Edwards Air Force Base down on Cape Cod?"

"Or if you live in a town that routinely sprayed carcinogenic foam on their kids!"

"Yup, it can affect their immune systems. Researchers also found out that kids who were exposed to PFAS may have more severe cases of diabetes and Covid-19."

"I've even heard anecdotal evidence that women exposed to high levels of PFAS can't nurse their babies because the PFAS interfere with their ability to produce milk."

"Haven't heard that. Must somehow interfere with the prolactin/pituitary pathway but I can't think how."

"The problem is that PFAS are chemical whack-a-moles. The government bans one PFA and the industry just starts using another one. Then it takes a decade to figure out that this new PFA was just as bad as the old one, and by that time the industry has started churning out even worse ones. The problem will only increase as we switch away from using fossil fuels."

"How come?"

"The chemical companies are looking for new ways they can sell the fossil fuels they have already invested in."

"Using Forever Chemicals to avoid freezing their assets."

"Yup, better living through chemistry."

"Yeah right!"

CHAPTER 34

The Counter Strike

Kharkiv, Ukraine
September 10, 2022

"It will be a long slow operation to grind down the enemy."

Zelensky's aide describing
the Counter Offensive in Kherson
August 30, 2022

"Hey Petra, can you get us down south so I can cover the counter offense?"

"No, but I can get you embedded into a small unit outside Kharkiv."

"Kharkiv? Why would I want to go to Kharkiv? Your defense ministry is saying all the action will be in Kherson."

"Don't believe everything you hear."

Three days later they were jogging down a shaded path outside Kharkiv when Svarog emerged out of the foliage with a small unit of camouflaged soldiers.

"Svarog, what are you doing here?" asked Gregor.

"Shh, the Russians are right up there. They have moved most of their tanks and artillery to the south. Dmitri what do you see on your drone?"

"Only one bedraggled detachment. They look tired and hungry."

"Just what we want to see. Call Victor and have him send in his tanks at full speed. We will follow to take any prisoners of war."

Fifteen minutes later the Ukrainian tanks had broken through the Russian front lines and Russian soldiers were scrambling to steal cars, bikes and civilian clothes to flee back into Russia. Gregor jotted down quick notes.

"So many cars are on the road they have formed a traffic jam reminiscent of the 40 miles of stalled tanks and trucks the world witnessed at the start of the war. Only this time other Russian soldiers are greeting them at the border with rifles ordering them back into battle.

In their wake the Russians have abandoned hundreds of jets, tanks, and trucks. It is ironic that the blitzkrieg that Putin had intended to subdue Kyiv in five days has become a 24 hour rout in which Ukraine has regained 300 villages and over a thousand square miles of territory that it had taken Russia seven months to capture.

It is like watching Tom Brady pick apart his opponent's defense then hitting a receiver deep in the end zone."

"Why do you Americans always use sports metaphors to write about war? European journalists never do that," said Petra reading over Gregor's shoulder.

"That's because we grow up playing football. You only have soccer."

"That is actually football. Much better sport!" said Svarog emphatically.

"And all you men have far too much testosterone!"

"I don't know- you don't drive like a testosterone deprived girl!"

"Better watch what you say if you want any action tonight."

"Ok, but Svarog, how did you know the counterattack would be in Kharkiv and not Kherson?'

"We learned that tactic from your rangers that trained us after the Crimean War. They taught us how to operate in these small units, move quickly and live off the land. They also taught us how to signal that we were going to strike in one area, so the enemy will redeploy their troops leaving a small spread-out group behind.

All we had to do was probe until we found their weak point,

then call in our tanks and artillery so they could smash through their lines and surround them."

"They must have been watching Tom Brady as well. But how did you get the information in all the press? I was monitoring BBC and CNN and reading about the Kherson offensive in the Times and the Guardian."

"I can answer that," said Petra. "It was all coordinated by Zelensky's office. For months all his aides talked about was how they were preparing for a long slow counter offensive in Kherson. Soon your pundits and military experts, and even their Russian counterparts were humble boasting that they were privy to inside information. It was all part of a well-coordinated campaign managed by Zelensky's former comedy writers."

"I would have loved to been in that writers' room."

"It was fun."

"What? You were there? Do you work for the CIA?"

"Nope, I'm just a Kyiv ambulance driver who has some friends. We are a small tightly knit community. Everyone knows everyone else."

"Since you are so well connected, what do you think will happen next?"

"Who knows? Maybe we will find another soft spot and advance; maybe we will rest and prepare for a long winter. Maybe Putin will do something stupid at one of the nuclear plants. What do you think, Svarog?"

"I've heard a unit trained by your Army Corps of Engineers has built a pontoon bridge across the Oskil River. Soon they will drive those scumbags out of Bilohorivika with of a broom. Step by step and centimeter by centimeter we will liberate Luhansk from the invaders."

"That would be a huge black eye for Putin. One of his key war aims was to gain full control of the region. What do you think Petra? Any more inside information?"

"Remember I'm just a simple ambulance driver. All I know is

that the momentum of the war has changed and Zele will push on until we win."

"I think you have a thing for Zelensky."

"We all have a thing for Zele!"

"Perhaps you have a thing for your Tom Brady," said Svarog punching Gregor's arm.

CHAPTER 35

Hurricane Ian

Cayo Costa, Florida
October 5, 2022

"Hey Leyla, look at this."

Ericka was watching a satellite loop of Hurricane Ian approaching Florida's southwest coast.

"My God, it looks like one of those computer generated storms you see in science fiction films. What are those flashes of light along the leading edge of the storm?"

"Lightning. Ian is actually a gyre of powerful thunderstorms swirling toward disaster."

"I dated an Ian once. That was a disaster too. Will you have to fly down to cover the aftermath?"

"Can't, all the flights have been cancelled. Even the trains aren't running. I'd been hoping we could stay up here and have the storms come to us.

But Ian will probably turn out to be the most damaging storm to ever hit Florida. It is right up there with Katrina, Sandy and Andrew. You up for a field trip?"

"What do you mean?"

'We can take your Tesla. Spend a night in Raleigh then continue on to Florida. It will take a little longer than flying but we won't use any gas."

"Do you think we'll find charging stations all the way down?"

"We should, and once we get to Florida, FEMA may let us use one of their generators. People are always helpful during emergencies."

"Hope so."

"Speaking of cars, think of how many have been ruined by the storm. You certainly won't want to buy a used car for several years."

"Why not?"

"Dealers can get them running long enough to sell 'em. But once water gets into a car's electrical system it's toast. I expect there will be over two million cars that will have to be replaced."

"If they are replaced with electric cars won't that be a big step forward?"

"It would be, if anyone could find any electric cars to sell. Unfortunately car makers don't have enough microchips and rare metals to meet the present demand."

"So, people will end up buying new gas powered cars to replace their old gas guzzling ones?"

"Yup, and a lot of those people had probably planned to buy an electric car in the next five years, but now they will wait for another ten years for their gas car to depreciate before buying an electric one. It could actually prove to be another huge step backwards."

———

A week later Ericka and Leyla were driving across the causeway onto Boca Grande.

"My parents brought me here as a kid. One day I was exploring around a bar in one of the old hotels and found the initials FWS on one of the tarpon scales tacked to the wall. Those are my father's initials, so I told him about it, but he said he hadn't caught the tarpon, his own father had.

He remembered it because my grandmother had been pissed that he had gotten stinking drunk with his fishing buddies on Useppa Island."

"Always knew our grandparents could out-party our generation any day of the week."

"But the good thing is that my father used to share a boat with a coastal geologist, and if we can find that guy, he should be able be able to ferry us across to Cayo Costa."

After a few wrong turns they met Ray Rodriquez, a deeply sun-tanned man with eyes squinty from peering for signs of tarpon in the sparkling waters of Boca Sound. As they cruised across the bay Ray pointed to the back of Cayo Costa.

"Unlike neighboring Sanibel and Captiva islands, nobody ever built any bridges or seawalls on Cayo Costa. That left the island free to fulfill its role as a natural barrier against major storms, so people could live behind its barrier beaches as the indigenous Calussa people had done hundreds of years before.

The lack of houses and such infrastructure made it easier for Florida to make the island into a state park in 1971.

Hurricane Charley tested the wisdom of that effort in 2004. It washed over Cayo Costa and on into Punta Gorda where it caused $25 billion in damages and left hundreds of people cooped up in FEMA trailers years after the storm had passed."

They watched as tendrils of fog lifted slowly off the island's nine miles of powdery white beaches.

"The island looks the way I remember it from 30 years ago."

"And probably 500 years before that."

"But I also remember when hundreds of Australian pines towered over the island. Now they have all been snapped in two."

"Yup the park rangers spent years trying to saw them down, but Charley did it in four minutes flat.

Now copses of native sea grapes are thriving in the sunlight where the pines used to be."

"I also remember seeing wild boar that slept under the palmetto palm groves, but then came out at sunset to root through the tidal flats for mole crabs, and feral horses that used to nuzzle visiting boaters."

"Yes, they removed all of them from the island, but alligators still lurk in the lagoon behind the swimming beach and of course the productive waters of the Gulf of Mexico still produce billions of shells that continue to wash up on the deceptively quiet beaches of Cayo Costa."

"Why do you say deceptive?"

"Because they still remain ready to absorb the powers of the next hurricane. They reflect the benefit of leaving a barrier beach in its natural state to stave off future storms. And the best way to do that was to make it into a public park.

Before Hurricane Ian, the park was thriving. Every day hundreds of visitors would arrive in their own boats or on small ferries and be taken across the island in modified golf carts driven by park volunteers. There they could spread out along a seven-mile-long pristine white Gulf of Mexico beach, or pitch a tent and spend a week fishing.

If you look carefully, you can see where the beach has rolled over itself as it moved inland during Hurricane Ian, and you can see some areas of slight erosion. But you'll never read anything about erosion on Cayo Costa because it has no houses or streets to wash away. So the island just remains as a pristine natural barrier island, ready to protect the mainland from the next storm."

"The last time I was here a friend of mine and I decided to drive across the state to compare Cayo Costa and its Calussa step pyramids built behind protective barrier beaches with Mar-a-Lago," said Ericka.

"Our original plan was to simply take a few pictures of the Italianate villa that sits only 4 feet above sea level on our country's most hurricane prone shore. But that was before anyone realized that the President intended to rule the country from his imperial looking villa.

So we didn't really know what to expect. I told my friend John that I would be more than happy if I could just take a few pictures from the car. Even if we were turned away I could probably write a story about the expensive security surrounding the new President who had residences in New York, Washington, New Jersey and Florida.

We had planned to park on the mainland and take pictures across the bayou but the bridge to Palm Beach was open so we decided to see if we could drive by the mansion itself.

No security was in sight, so we drove down a side street where a cop car was parked. We figured we could ask if it was ok to take a few photographs but the car was empty, so we parked and walked.

The adjacent street was separated from Mar-a-Lago by a high hedge, but a path led through the vegetation to an open gate. I walked through the gate and started to take photos of a huge American flag flapping over the red-tiled building. A couple explained that the city of Palm Beach had tried to restrict the height of the oversized flag but had been overridden -- by executive order no doubt.

Since nobody was around, I took a few more steps and suddenly realized I was standing on the front lawn. A groundskeeper eventually came along and told us that it was a private resort and we would have to leave. We said we were sorry and walked back to our car.

Nobody had bothered to ask for credentials or just what the hell we thought we were doing."

"You were lucky you weren't in the crosshairs of a SWAT team sitting on the roof," said Leyla.

"Don't think so. There seemed to be a total lack of security."

"A few days ago, CNN did a story about the Mar-a-Lago security leaks that included an aerial shot of the compound," said Ray.

"Yup saw it, and there was the copse of vegetation we hid in before stepping out onto the front lawn!"

What fascinates me how we are drawn to such short-term people driven stories and away from a long-term ones like sea level rise."

"I think it is in our genes."

"Yes, that and the belief that our monuments to powerful leaders will last forever."

"I image the Calussas thought the same thing."

CHAPTER 36

Babcock Ranch

Charlotte County and Lee County, Florida
October 12, 2022

A week later Leyla was driving through the remains of Fort Myers where two million people had lost their power and over a hundred elderly residents had drowned in their own homes by Ian's sixteen-foot storm surge.

"Everything is flattened, I can't believe this devastation. How are you going to write about it?"

"I'm not. Everyone is going to be writing about the destruction of Fort Myers and how we should stop placing cities in the path of hurricanes.

Straight ahead is a place called Babcock Ranch, a planned community only 12 miles from Fort Myers. But there, nobody was killed, nobody lost power and none of the buildings were badly damaged."

"How did it get such a weird name?"

"It was named for a Mr. Babcock."

"You mean like the bad guy banker in Auntie Mame?"

"Same name, different guy. This Babcock was a Midwestern lumberman who brought 93,000 acres stretching across a great swath of Southwest Florida. He took over stewardship of the property, removing invasive species, replenishing depleted forests and introducing ostrich and alligator farming."

"Hmm that could be a pretty grisly closed system."

"It could, but in 2006 the property was transferred to the state of Florida to be held as conservation land while an additional 18,000 acres of land went to Syd Kitson, a former professional football player who had a dream of building the world's first all solar powered town."

"So why did it survive when so many cities and towns were flattened?"

"First of all, they were twelve miles inland on land that is twenty-five feet above sea level. And all the houses were designed to withstand a Category 4 hurricane with 145 mph winds. Plus, there's a system of dams and holding ponds to retain water during dry periods, and the streets are designed to act like rivers to keep water from flowing into residents' basements during storms."

"Sounds like they thought of almost everything."

"Their biggest advantage is that all of the 4,600 residents get their electricity from a 900-acre solar field with 700,000 panels, none of which were seriously damaged by Ian."

"Impressive."

"Yes, they fared so well that they were able to keep a shelter open in one of their community schools powered by solar energy. Nobody had expected to be able to use the shelter because its generator hadn't been delivered. It turned out that it was the only shelter in the entire region that still had power after the storm."

"I imagine they will be getting a lot of calls from folks in Fort Myers who lost their homes."

CHAPTER 37

A Bridge Too Far

Kanapa Restaurant
Kyiv, Ukraine
October 13, 2022

Petra and Gregor sipped thick black coffee at the Kanapa Restaurant in Kyiv.

"So which one of your important friends are we going to meet today?"

"You've already met him."

"Who, Zelensky?"

"Nope more important than Zele."

Just at that moment their waiter sat down beside them and dipped down his surgical mask."

"Svarog! I didn't recognize you!"

"Good! That's the point isn't it?"

"Hmm shall we order the Chicken Kiev?"

"If you want, but I'm having the rabbit meat borscht. We eat it on maneuvers if we can find any rabbits after the Russkies retreat."

Petra chimed in, "I'd recommend the root salad with a cheese topping and cherry dumplings for dessert."

"You seem awfully happy today Svarog. You didn't happen to have anything to do with blowing up the Kerch Straits Bridge did you?"

"Oh no, no. I'm just happy. It's President Putin's birthday! It was a nice present, though, don't you think?"

"Yes, tell us about it."

"Well, we had to coordinate with our partisans in Russia to figure exactly when their echelon of fuel filled railroad cars would be on the bridge over our Ukrainian territorial waters. That way

Putin couldn't say we were attacking mother Russia. Your State Department also warned us about stepping over that line."

"Yes, the CIA is in a lot of trouble for forecasting that Russia would capture Kyiv in five days."

"What about the driver of the truck. Did he trigger the explosion himself?" asked Petra.

"Who says the driver was a 'he' and who says there was a driver at all?"

"You mean your techies rigged up a self-driving truck?"

"And who says there was a truck? We don't believe in suicide bombers, but why use a self-driving truck when divers could place explosives under the bridge timed to go off at 6 am when few civilians would be around, and exactly when the railroad cars would be opposite the car and truck bridge."

"Did you time it to happen on Putin's birthday?"

"Could have."

"But have you pushed him too far?"

"We have put the Russians in a real bind. There is no way they can get enough fuel and ammunition to their soldiers in Kherson, and for their collaborators to flee back to Russia. They realize this is also just the beginning of our taking back Crimea."

When will you do that?"

"Ah Gregor my friend, always asking questions you know I can't answer."

"That's my job."

"I can tell you it will come when and where they least expect it. We have lots of other tricks up our sleeves."

"The Russians are what we call punch drunk in America. They don't know where the next attack will come from."

"I like that, punch drunk. I'll have to tell my colleagues.

Now all Putin can do is bomb civilians and all that will do is convince the West to give us air defense weapons. He is running low on cruise missiles so he is using Iranian drones."

"What if he uses tactical nuclear weapons?"

"If he does he knows, or should know, that NATO will rain

down Tomahawk missiles on every soldier and installation still in Ukraine."

"You guys thought of everything didn't you?"

"Almost, but I wish we could have taken out that railroad bridge as well as the truck one."

CHAPTER 38

"We Are in Trouble!"

Cromwell Institute
Toronto, Canada
October 19, 2022

Leyla listened as Ericka and Sylvia talked shop on their way to see the director of the Cromwell Institute in Toronto.

"Neurology was my favorite course in med school. But you know I flunked it the first time I took the exam."

"How did that happen?"

"The weekend before the exam I developed a lump so I went to the on-call resident who examined my neck and said I could possibly have a sarcoma."

"My God, what did you do?"

"I worried so much I couldn't study, so I went to my professor and blurted out, 'Doctor Braun, I'm so sorry to bother you. You know I love neurology, but I had a sarcoma over the weekend and couldn't study.'"

"He simply laughed and said, 'I must be a good teacher because my students always seem to develop symptoms of the diseases I have just discussed in class. Just go home, don't worry about your sarcoma, that's seems to have disappeared, study hard, and retake the test in two weeks.'"

"How did you do?"

"Aced it."

"Of course, you did!"

"On rounds we sometimes had patients with hallucinations of children standing quietly in the room."

"That must have been unnerving!"

"I thought so at first, but after a while I started to ask the patients if the hallucinations bothered them and most said they didn't.

We had one woman who kept seeing children sitting on the edge of her bed staring at her. She said she knew the children weren't real but she felt more comfortable changing her clothes in the bathroom just in case."

"No need for any fancy meds for that one."

"Yeah, but we had another elderly patient named Lucy. She was very wealthy and was visited every day by her friend Irving who always came in draped head to toe in mink and covered with fine diamonds.

They laughed all the time, but Lucy kept complaining that she saw mice scurrying across her room every night. We assured her there were no mice and explained she was just having hallucinations and started her on Haldol."

"The antipsychotic medication?"

"Yeah, the next morning she was slurring her words pretty badly but she could just get out that she was still seeing mice. So we doubled her dose."

"Oh no!"

"Yup, the third day she could barely talk but she groggily explained that Irving had smuggled in her new Polaroid camera under his coat, and she had taken some pictures she wanted us to see. Sure enough there were those damn mice running all over her private room."

"What did you do?"'

"We called the exterminator and took her off Haldol."

"Of course!"

"It was an object lesson in always listening to your patients."

"What about this new Scottish study that shows that one out of every twenty people with long term Covid can continue to have neurological problems 18 months after they get it?"

"It shows we're in real trouble. Up to 23 million Americans are affected by long Covid, including a million that can't work because of brain fog, fatigue and mental deterioration."

"Oh, so that's what I have!"

Leyla swung into the Cromwell Institute where a guard ushered Ericka and Sylvia down a long hall to Dr. Weber's lab.

"Do you mind coffee in a beaker? We never use cups in the Cromwell."

"Of course, that's fine. I understand we might be seeing the beginnings of a new paradigm for our understanding of brain diseases."

Ericka added, "Science writers are always interested in paradigm shifts. We don't necessarily seek them out but it is important to be able to recognize the real thing, instead headlines that tout old information as if it heralded a startling new discovery."

"Yes, well for the past sixteen years we Alzheimer researchers have been in a rut. The prevailing model has been that Alzheimer is associated with beta amyloid tangles, so scientists have been working diligently to find ways to break up those tangles.

But a few months ago, Science magazine reported that the seminal beta amyloid paper was riddled with fraudulent data.

So, we are working on a new model that looks at Alzheimer disease as an autoimmune disease."

"How does that work?"

"When a virus or bacterium infects someone's brain, the brain's immune system swings into action using a series of immunological proteins including beta amyloid, to fight the infection. But the antibodies can't differentiate between the antigenic markers of cell membranes of the bacteria and the neuronal cell markers, so they start attacking both the brain and the bacteria. This could lead to a cascade of cell function loss leading to dementia."

"So, you're saying Alzheimer disease might be an autoimmune disease like rheumatoid arthritis."

"Exactly but unlike RA, steroid-based therapies don't seem to work to treat Alzheimer disease."

"What will work?"

"We believe that by targeting other immunological pathways we can discover an effective treatment."

"Pretty exciting."

"Another theory is that Alzheimer disease is a disease of mitochondria."

"Aren't those the structures that convert oxygen and food into energy?" asked Ericka.

"Yes, evolutionary biologists believe that about 1.5 billion years ago, an ancient organism ingested an oxygen consuming bacterium but instead of being killed the bacteria became incorporated into the organism's intracellular structures giving it the ability to use oxygen and glucose to produce energy. We are all the progeny of that early organism."

"And can't symbiosis also be a form of parasitism?"

"Yes, so some people think that Alzheimer disease is the end-result of an infection that comes from ingesting bacteria that attack the brain setting off an autoimmune response."

"It sounds something like the primitive immune system of horseshoe crabs," said Ericka."

"How so?"

"They developed an immune system to protect themselves from the membranes of Gram-negative bacteria."

"Interesting. We think the beta amyloid cells could be part of a similar system that can go into overdrive and trigger an autoimmune response."

"Similar thing happens to a horseshoe crab when it is overwhelmed by bacteria."

"You'll have to excuse Ericka, she sees everything in terms of horseshoe crabs," said Sylvia.

"It's how I understand things."

"Not a bad disease model actually."

"Or she could be on the spectrum!"

Everyone laughed a little nervously.

"Fascinating theories Dr. Weber. Thank you so much for your time. Good luck with your work."

"Thank you. Put a penny under our Buddha statue on your way out. It brings us good results with our experiments. It should work for your writing as well."

"We hope so!"

CHAPTER 39

Editorial Meeting

Boston Globe
December 15, 2022

"Prediction is Very Difficult,
Particularly About the Future."
Niels Bohr
Quoting an old Danish Saying

Finbar opened the December Zoom session at 9am. "Good morning everyone. This has been a remarkable year. Time for our regular roundup, what can you say about your beats and what do you think will happen next year?"

Ericka: "Oh great, our annual science fiction feature."

Finbar: "OK Ericka why don't you start? What happened at COP27?"

Ericka: "What can I say? I used a year's worth of fuel to fly to Sharm El Sheik and spent most of my time trying to find coffee and sandwiches in the sprawling venue. It was the most chaotic conference I have ever been to. The president of the conference would hold late night meetings then only show diplomats snippets of the text the next morning."

Sylvia: "But didn't they set up a fund to pay poor countries for damages caused by climate change?"

Ericka: "Yeah and they spent two weeks debating whether to call it reparations, compensation, or money for loss and damages."

Gregor: "So, will we end up paying China even though it spews more carbon into the air than any other country?"

Ericka: "Well that's a double-edged sword. China does emit more carbon dioxide than any other nation, but it is also classified as a developing nation so it could still be eligible to receive loss and damage funds."

Sylvia: "But haven't the US and Europe emitted much more carbon dioxide than China over the years and isn't it those emissions that are causing today's global warming?"

Ericka: "True and it remains doubtful that the world will be able to stick to its goal of only allowing the planet to heat up by 1.5 degrees."

Sylvia: "What will that mean?"

Ericka: "It means you can say goodbye to most of the cities we love and live in. Several of the countries represented at the conference will simply disappear off the face of the earth and at least 200 million people will be flooded out of their homes even if we stop all emissions tomorrow."

Sylvia: "And the amazing thing is that those people live in exactly the same places with the highest growth rates. Places like Pakistan, India, Nigeria. It doesn't make sense, why would anyone move into such flood prone areas?"

Ericka: "Because those are also the most productive areas, so people want to move there to farm and fish."

Sylvia: "We see the same sort of thing in this country. Look what happens after a storm washes a home into the ocean. A developer swoops in, buys up the cheap lot then builds a new house on exactly the same footprint as before."

Ericka: "And his real estate agent will only show the house in the summer when the ocean is calm and peaceful. And there will always be some poor slob from the Mid-West, if not the Middle East, who will gladly pay to live beside the ocean, and never be the wiser until he is wiped out by the next storm."

Finbar: "Can't you give us some good news Ericka?"

Ericka: "Of course the biggest story of this year and probably of the entire 21st century occurred at the Lawrence Livermore Lab. That's where all the really smart dudes are."

Finbar: "What happened?"

Ericka: "On December 5th, 192 lasers bombarded two hydrogen atoms to 100 times the density of lead and at over 100 million degrees Celsius. That fused the two hydrogen atoms into an atom of helium, which produced enough energy to boil about ten pots of coffee.

In making the announcement Energy Secretary Jennifer Granholm said, 'This is one of the most important scientific feats of the 21st century or as the President might say, and I think he probably did say, this is a BFD'"

Gregor: "Ten pots of coffee doesn't sound like such a BFD to me."

Ericka: "Don't be so obtuse Gregor. The crucial thing is that the researchers were able to produce about 50% more energy than they put in. When they solve all the technical and engineering problems fusion technology should be able to supply an almost inexhaustible supply of cheap green energy with zero carbon emissions."

Sylvia: "A game changer. When will this happen?"

Ericka: "The White House is saying in a decade. I'd say more like 50 years. Another way of looking at it that our generation and our children's generation will continue to see more global warming, but if nuclear fusion and carbon extraction work, our great great grandchildren might see things start to improve.

The other important thing about this achievement is that it was produced with lasers. Most of the other government and privately supported labs have been using magnets."

Finbar: "Which do you think will win out?"

Ericka: "It doesn't really matter. What matters is that you have two technologies competing against each other, which gives humanity two potential ways to solve our climate crisis."

Finbar: "That was excellent Ericka, a nice way to go into the New Year. But how do things look in Ukraine, Gregor?"

Gregor: "It looks like both sides are settling in for a long cold winter. It is clear that Russia intends to continue to brutalize both civilians and their infrastructure.

For a while it looked like the Ukrainians were going to move rapidly north to the Nova Kakhovka causeway where they could repair its slightly damaged bridge, cross the Dnieper and liberate more southerly cities. But they ran into hundreds of new Russian recruits that kept coming after their comrades were mowed down. But they are keeping the Ukrainians tied down so they can't attack other areas."

Finbar: "But aren't the Russians in danger of running out of ammunition and missiles faster than the Ukrainians who are being supplied by the West?"

Gregor: "They do have Iran, who has been supplying them with their highly effective kamikaze drones. Iran has its own problems but will probably keep shipping Russia more drones.

It all comes down to logistics and momentum. Ukraine has 'em and Russia doesn't. That has allowed the Ukrainians to methodically cut the Russians off from their supplies then make lightning strikes to recapture territory Russia stole eight years ago."

Finbar: "Is it possible Ukraine can capture Crimea?"

Gregor: "Not only possible but likely if they can survive winter and continue their methodical advance in the spring. Remember Crimea is about the size of Massachusetts and is loved as much as Cape Cod."

Sylvia: "But, how can you say that with such certainty?"

Gregor: "I can't. Nobody really knows for sure. This winter is going to be horrific but there are signs that Russia is running out of ammunition. Zelensky could even be saying Ukraine plans to recapture Crimea to scare Putin into a diplomatic solution."

Finbar: "But isn't a bit of caution in order? Couldn't Putin use an attack on Crimea to rally his lagging domestic support?"

Gregor: "He could but he is still stuck with a demoralized army and lousy logistics. But one thing is clear, if Ukraine does capture Crimea the first thing they will do is tear down the Kerch Straits Bridge."

Sylvia: "Didn't you write somewhere that the Russians should be careful about burning their bridges? Doesn't the same thing apply to the Ukrainians?"

Gregor: "That was a week ago, this is today!"

Finbar: "So much for the fog of war. OK, Sylvia can you peer into your crystal ball and tell us what to expect on the health front?"

Sylvia: "On the health front? Well, we have to contend with the fog of billions of viruses rapidly evolving to circumvent our immune systems and our shiny new technologies to contain them.

But the main story is still Covid. Although the number of cases were at an all-time low, health experts expect them to climb again now that people are getting together for the holidays."

Ericka: "So we can't start getting free lunches in the cafeteria again."

Gregor: "Perhaps we can hire away that fancy chef over at Google."

"Ericka: "Unlikely. Those guys will kill for their perks."

Finbar: "Sylvia, what about the protests in China?"

Sylvia: "That's a tough one. Scientifically and medically their zero Covid policy worked but people became fed up with the lock-downs and how they were hurting their economy."

Finbar: "And the global economy because some of the worst riots are in Zengzhou where they make most of the world's microchips."

Sylvia: "China's problem is that they don't have a backup plan. Their vaccines are suboptimal so if they drop their zero Covid policy the virus could spread around the world again.

But my biggest long-term fear for our country are the anti-vaxxers. Despite the fact that our messenger RNA vaccine saved 20 million people from dying, fewer that 50% got boosted and it is likely that vaccine hesitancy and fatigue will spill over into other vaccines in the U.S. and other countries."

Finbar: "Why?"

Sylvia: "It's complicated. But part of it stems from the fact that American consumers tend to view vaccines like dietary supplements or over the counter medication, so they believe it is up to them to decide on the efficacy of vaccines rather than to listen to their doctor's advice."

Finbar: "It is all part of this new don't trust science don't trust experts mentality. In fact can't we use that as a theme for all of our end of the year stories?"

Sylvia: "Maybe we can even make a small difference."

Finbar: "Anyone have trips planned for the holidays?"

Ericka: "Leyla and I plan to fly to Costa Rica to recharge our batteries. I hope you all have equally wonderful vacations and come back ready to continue improve ourselves and our planet!"

Gregor: "Wow Ericka, I didn't know you had it in you. Leyla must be improving your view on life."

Ericka: "As is Petra doing the same for yours Gregor!"

Finbar: "OK you hard bitten journalists. Enjoy the holidays and be ready to get back out there next year to do our jobs."

-END-

ABOUT THE AUTHOR

William Sargent is a NOVA consultant and award winning author of 28 books about science and the environment.

You can learn more about Bill at WilliamSargent.net

And find more titles by Bill at https://www.amazon.com/stores/William-Sargent/author/B001HCXE3U

Made in the USA
Columbia, SC
05 March 2023

13228353R00088